Sharon Kendrick

THE PATERNITY CLAIM

EXPECTING!

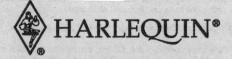
HARLEQUIN®

TORONTO • NEW YORK • LONDON
AMSTERDAM • PARIS • SYDNEY • HAMBURG
STOCKHOLM • ATHENS • TOKYO • MILAN • MADRID
PRAGUE • WARSAW • BUDAPEST • AUCKLAND

To Maria das Gracas Fish of the Brazilian Embassy,
London, with thanks for showing me how vibrant
and exuberant Brazilian people can be.

ISBN 0-373-12371-X

THE PATERNITY CLAIM

First North American Publication 2004.

"Can you understand why I ran to England, Paulo?"

"Yes, I can." He nodded his head slowly. "But you've compromised me now, haven't you, *querida?* Your father is convinced that I sired your baby. And to tell him otherwise would risk the kind of commotion you're anxious to avoid."

"So what do I do?"

His eyes glittered as he considered her question, the memory of her kiss still sweet on his mouth. "You stay here. With me. And after the baby is born, well, then…" He shrugged as he gave his rare and sexy smile.

"Then what?" Isabella questioned slowly. "What exactly are you suggesting?"

"Why, then we could enjoy our mutual passion, Bella," he purred, seeing the darkening in her eyes. "After all, why should I take all of the responsibility of impending paternity, but with none of the corresponding pleasure? Live here. With me. And we will become lovers."

Lovers.

CHAPTER ONE

COME on, come *on*! With a frustration born out of fear, Isabella jammed her thumb on the doorbell one last time and let it ring and ring, long enough to wake the dead—and certainly long enough to rouse the occupant of the elegant London townhouse. Just in case he hadn't heard her the first time round.

But there was nothing other than the sound of the bell echoing and her hand fell to her side as she forced herself to accept the unthinkable. That he wasn't there. That she would have to make a return journey—if she could summon up the courage to come here for a second time.

And then the door was flung open with a force of a powerhouse—and one very angry man stood looking down at her, his crisp dark head still damp and shining from the shower. Tiny droplets of water sparkled among the brown-black waves of his hair. Lit from behind, it almost looked as though he were wearing a halo—though the expression on his face was about as unangelic as you could get.

His black eyes glittered with irritation at this unwelcome intrusion and Isabella felt her heart begin to race. Because even in her current nerve-jangled state of crisis his physical impact was like a shock to the senses.

He was wearing nothing but a deep blue towel which was slung low around narrow olive hips and came to midway down a pair of impressively muscled thighs. Half of his chin was covered with shaving foam and in his hand he held an old-fashioned cut-throat razor which glinted silver beneath the gleam of the chandelier overhead.

Isabella swallowed. She had seen his magnificent body in swimming trunks many, many times—but never quite so *intimately* naked.

'Yes?' he snapped, in an accent which did not match the Brazilian ancestry of his looks and a tone which suggested that he was not the kind of man to tolerate interruption. 'Where's the fire?'

'Hello, Paulo,' she said quietly.

For the split second before his brain started making sense of the information it was receiving, Paulo stared impatiently at the woman who was standing on his doorstep looking up at him with such wary expectation in her eyes.

He ignored the sensual, subliminal messages which her sultry beauty was hot-wiring to his body, because his overriding impression was how ridiculously *exotic* she looked.

She wore a brand-new raincoat which came right down to a pair of slender ankles, so that only her face was on show. A face covered with droplets of rain from the summer shower, her dark hair plastered to her head. Huge, golden-brown eyes—like lumps of old and expensive amber—were fringed with the longest, blackest lashes he had ever seen. Her lips were lush, and unpainted. And trembling, he thought with a sudden frown. Trembling…

She looked like a lost and beautiful waif, and a warning bell clanged deep within the recesses of his mind. He knew her, and yet somehow he also knew that she shouldn't be here.

Wrong place. Definitely.

'Hello,' he murmured, while his mind raced ahead to slot her into her rightful place.

'Why, Paulo,' she said softly, thinking for one unimaginable moment that he actually didn't *recognise* her. 'I wrote and told you that I was coming—didn't you get my letter?'

The moment she spoke a complete sentence, the facts fell into place. Her accent matched her dark, Latin looks—although her English was as fluent as his. The almond-shaped eyes set in a skin which was the seamless colour of cappuccino. The quiet gleam of black hair which lay plastered against her skull by the rain.

The last time he had seen her, she had been standing illuminated by the brilliant sunshine of a South American day. Her silk shirt had been stretched with outrageous provocation over her ripe, young breasts and there had been the dark stain of sweat beneath her arms. He had wanted her in that moment. And maybe before that, too.

Resolutely he pushed that particular thought away, even as his eyes began to soften with affection. No wonder he hadn't recognised her, against the grey and teaming backdrop of an English summer day, looking cold and hunched. And dejected.

'Isabella! *Meu Deus!* I can't believe it!' he exclaimed, and he leaned forward to kiss her on each cheek. The normal and formal Latin American greeting, but rather bizarre and unsettling—considering that he was wearing next to nothing. He noticed that although she offered him each cool cheek, she shrank away from any contact with his bare skin. And he offered up a silent prayer of thanks.

'Come *in*,' he urged. 'Are you on your own?'

'M-my own?'

He frowned. 'Is your father here with you?'

Isabella swallowed. 'No. No, he's not.'

He opened the door wider and she stepped inside.

'Why on earth didn't you tell me you were coming?' he demanded. 'This is so—'

'Unexpected?' she put in quickly. 'Yes, I know it is.' She nodded her head in rapid agreement—but then she was prepared to agree to almost anything if he would only help her. She didn't know how—she just knew that Paulo Dantas was the kind of man who could cope with anything that life threw at him. 'But you got my letter, didn't you?' she asked.

He nodded thoughtfully. It had been an oddly disjointed letter mentioning that she might be coming to England sometime soon. But he had thought of soon in terms of years. He certainly wasn't expecting her *now*, not yet—when she was still at university. 'Yeah, I got your letter. But that was a couple of months back.'

She had written it the day she had found out for sure. The day she realised the trouble she was in. 'I shouldn't have just burst in on you like this. I tried ringing, but the line was engaged and so I knew you were here and I...I...'

Her voice faded away, unsure where to go from here. In her mind she had practised what she was going to say over and over again, but the disturbing sight of a near-naked Paulo had startled her, and the carefully rehearsed words were stubbornly refusing to come. Not, she thought grimly, that it was the kind of thing you could just blurt out on somebody's doorstep.

'I thought it might be nice to surprise you,' she finished lamely.

'Well, you've certainly done that.'

But Isabella saw his sudden swift, assessing frown. 'I'm sorry, I've come at an awkward time—'

'Well, I can't deny that I was busy—' he murmured, as the hand which wasn't holding the razor strayed down to touch the towel at his hips, as if checking that the knot remained secure. 'But I can dress and shave in a couple of minutes.'

'Or I could come back later?'

'What, send you away when you've travelled thousands of miles?' He shook his crisp, dark head. 'No, no! I'm intrigued to discover what brings Isabella Fernandes to England in such dramatic style.'

Isabella paled, as she tried to imagine what his reaction would be when she told him her momentous piece of news. But there was one more obstacle to overcome before she dared accept his offer of hospitality. What she had to tell him was for his ears alone. 'Is Eduardo here?'

And some sort of transformation occurred. A face which was fundamentally hard and uncompromising underwent a dramatic softening, and a smile of pure pleasure lifted the corners of his mouth—making him look even more outrageously handsome than he had done before.

'Eduardo? Unfortunately, no.' The mouth curved into heart-stopping grin. 'Ten-year-old boys prefer to play football with their friends rather than keep their father company—and my son is no exception. He won't be back until later. A—' Inexplicably, he hesitated. 'A friend of mine is bringing him home.'

'Oh.' The word came out with just the right amount of disappointment, but Isabella wondered if the relief showed on her face. She also wondered who the friend was, as she quickly wiped a raindrop off her cheek.

Paulo watched the jerky little movement of her hand. She seemed nervous, he thought. Excessively nervous. Not a quality he had ever associated with Isabella. She could outshoot most men—and ride a horse with more grace than he had ever seen in another human being. He had watched her grow from child to woman—in the condensed, snap-shot way you did when you only saw someone once a year.

'You'll see him later. Come on—take off that wet raincoat. You're shivering.'

She was shivering for a variety of reasons—and coldness was the least of them.

'Th-thank you.' She stood blinking beneath the glow of the artificial light which danced overhead, frozen by the strangeness of this new environment. And the fact that Paolo was standing next to her, still wearing next to nothing, a faint drift of lemon about him—as indolently at ease with his semi-naked state as if he had been wearing a three-piece suit.

With numb fingers, she began fumbling with the buttons of her coat and Paulo felt the strongest urge to unbutton it for her, as you would a child—except that the first lush glimpse of her T-shirted breasts reinforced the fact that she was anything but a child. And that if he didn't put some decent clothes on in a minute...

'I can't believe you didn't buy an umbrella, Bella?' he teased, in an attempt to divert his uncomfortable thoughts. 'Did nobody tell you that in England it rains and rains? And then it rains some more—even in summer!'

'I thought I'd buy one when I got here, and then I...well, I forgot,' she finished lamely, although an umbrella had been the very last thing on her mind. She had spent weeks and weeks just wearing her father down.

Telling him that it was *her* life and her decision. And that lots of people of her age dropped out of university. She had told him that it wasn't the end of the world, but the look on his face had told her otherwise. Isabella shivered. And he didn't the know the half of it.

He felt the slight tremor in her body as he tugged the cuff of her jacket over her wrist and hung the garment on a peg above a radiator. 'There. You're dry underneath. Come into the sitting room.'

Reaction set in. He was letting her stay. Her teeth started to chatter but she clamped them shut. 'Thank you.'

'Need a towel for your hair?' he asked, shooting her a quick glance. 'Or maybe borrow a sweater?'

'No. Honestly. I'll be fine.' But she didn't feel fine. Her limbs felt stiff and icy as he led her along a wide, deep hallway and into a large, high-ceilinged room, its cool, classic lines made warmly informal by the pulsating colours he had chosen.

Isabella looked around her. It was a very *Latino* colour scheme.

The walls were painted a rich, burnt orange colour and deepest red and covered with vibrant pictures—there was one she instantly recognised as the work of an up-and-coming Brazilian painter. Two giant sofas were strewn with scatter cushions and a low table contained magazines and papers and a book about football. Dotted around the place were photographs of a young boy in various stages of growing up—Paulo's son—and a black and white studio portrait of a cool, beautiful blonde, her pale shining hair held close to a little baby. And that, Isabella knew, was Elizabeth—Paulo's wife.

'Make yourself comfortable,' he instructed, 'while I

get dressed and then I'll make you some coffee—how does that sound?'

'Coffee would be lovely,' she replied automatically.

Paulo went back upstairs and into the bathroom to finish shaving and frowned at himself in the mirror. Something was different about her. Something. And not just that she'd put on a little weight. Something had changed. Something indefinable... And it was something more than the dramatic sexual flowering he had noticed a few short months ago. He moved the blade swiftly over the curved line of his jaw.

He had known her for ever. Their fathers had been friends—and the friendship had survived separation when Paulo's father had eventually settled in England, the home of his new wife. Paulo had been born in Brazil, but had been brought to live in London at the age of six and his father had insisted he make an annual pilgrimage back to his homeland. It was a pilgrimage Paulo had carried on after the deaths of his parents and the birth of his own son.

Every year, just before Carnival erupted in a blaze of colour, he and Eduardo would travel to the Fernandes ranch for a couple of weeks and Paulo had seen Isabella grow up before his eyes.

He had watched with interest as the little girl had blossomed to embrace the whole spectrum of teenage behaviour. She had been stubborn and sassy and sulky, like all teenage girls. By seventeen she had begun to develop a soft, voluptuous beauty all of her own, but at seventeen she had still seemed so *young*. Certainly to him. Even at eighteen and nineteen she had seemed a different generation to a man who was, after all, a decade older, already widowed and with a young son of his own.

But something had happened to Isabella in her twentieth year. In the blinking of an eye, her sexuality had exploded into vibrant, throbbing life and Paulo had been touched by it; his senses had been scorched by it.

He had lifted her down from her horse and there had been a split-second of suspended movement as he held her in his arms. He had felt the indentation of her waist and the dampness of her shirt as it clung to her sweat-sheened skin. Their laughter had stilled and he had seen the suddening darkening of her pupils as she had looked into his eyes with a hunger which had matched his own.

Desire. Potent as any drug.

And his conscience had made him want no part of it.

He removed the towel from his hips, staring down at himself with flushed disbelief as he observed the first stirring of arousal. He scowled. Because that was the whole damned trouble with sexual attraction—once you'd felt it, you could never go back to how it was before. His easy, innocent relationship with Isabella had been annihilated in that one brief flash of desire. *That* was what was different.

His mouth twisted as he crumpled up the towel and hurled it with vicious accuracy into the linen basket, then gingerly stepped into a pair of silken boxer shorts.

Isabella wandered distractedly around the sitting room, going over in her head what she was going to say to him, forcing herself to be strong because only her strength would sustain her through this. 'Paulo, I'm...'

No, she couldn't come straight out with it. She would have to lead in with a casual yet suitably serious statement. No matter that deep down she felt like howling her heart out with shock and disbelief...because indulging her feelings at the moment would benefit no one. 'Paulo, I need your help...'

She heard the jangle of cups and looked up, relieved

to find that he had covered up with a pair of jeans and a T-shirt. On his chin sat a tiny, glistening bead of scarlet and it drew her attention like a magnet.

He saw the amber brilliance of her eyes as she stared at him and felt the dull pounding of his heart in response. 'What is it?' he asked huskily.

'You've cut yourself,' she whispered, and the bright sight of his blood seemed like a portent of what was to come.

Paulo frowned, lifting a fingertip to his chin. 'Where?'

'To the right. Yes. There.'

The finger brushed against the newly shaven surface and drew it away; he looked at it with a frown. Had his hand been shaking? He couldn't remember the last time he'd cut his face. 'Right,' he said, absently licking the finger with a gesture which was unintentionally erotic. 'Coffee.'

She tried for the light touch but it wasn't easy when all the time she felt the weight of the great burden she carried. 'I haven't had a decent cup since I left home.'

'I can imagine.' He smiled.

She watched as he slid onto the sofa, moving with the inborn grace of an alley cat. Back home they always called him *gato*, and it was easy to understand why. The word in Portuguese meant 'cat' but it also meant a sexy and beautiful man—and no one in the world could deny that Paulo Dantas was just that.

Tall, dark and statuesque, he was a matchless mix of English mother and Brazilian father. His was a spectacular face, with an arrogant sweep of cheekbones which could have been sculpted from some gold-tinted stone and hooded eyes more black than brown. The luscious mouth hinted at a deeply sensual nature, its starkly defined curves making it look as if it had been created to inflict both pleasure and pain in equal measures.

She took the coffee that he offered her with a hand which was threatening to tremble. 'Thank you.'

This was *crazy*, thought Paulo, as he observed her unfamiliar, frozen smile and her self-conscious movements. It was like being in a room with a stranger. What the hell had happened to her? 'How is your father?' he enquired politely.

'He—he's very well, thank you.' She tried to lift the coffee cup to her lips but now her fingers were shaking so much that she was obliged to put it down with a clatter. 'He says to say hello to you.'

'Say hello back,' he said evenly, but it was difficult to concentrate when that shaky movement made the lush curves of her body move so uninhibitedly beneath the T-shirt.

Isabella wondered if she was going mad with imagining, or had his gaze just flickered over her breasts? She wondered how much he had seen—and Paulo was an astute man, no one could deny that. Had he begun to guess at her secret already? Unobstrusively she glanced down at herself.

No, she was safe. The hot-pink T-shirt was relatively loose and the matching jeans were far from skin-tight. Nothing clung to the contours of her body. And besides, there was no visible bump yet. Nothing to show that there was a baby on the way, bar the aching new fullness of her breasts and the sudden nausea which could strike her at any time. And frequently did.

She tried a smile, but felt it wobble on her lips. 'I expect you're wondering why I'm here.'

At last! 'Well, the thought *had* crossed my mind,' he said, managing to turn curiosity into a teasing little comment. 'People don't just turn up from Brazil unannounced—not as a rule. Not without phoning first. And it's a pretty long way from Vitória da Conquista.'

Isabella turned her head to glance out of the uncurtained window into the rain-lashed sky. It certainly was. Back home the temperature would be as warm as kisses, the land caressed by a soft and sultry breeze.

'And shouldn't you be at college? It's still term-time, isn't it?'

She started to tell the story, though not the whole story. Not yet. 'Actually, I've dropped out of college.'

His body shifted imperceptibly from relaxed to watchful. 'Why?' he drawled coldly. 'Is that what every fashionable student is doing this year?'

She didn't like the way his mouth had flattened, nor the chilly displeasure in his eyes. 'No, not exactly.'

'Then why?' he demanded. 'Don't you know how important qualifications are in an insecure world? What are you planning to do that's so important that it can't wait until the end of your course?'

She opened her mouth to tell him about her dreams of travelling, of seeing a world outside the one she had grown up in—and then she remembered, and hastily shut it again. Because that would never happen now. She had forfeited her right to do any of that. 'I had to...get away.'

Paulo frowned. Her anxiety was almost palpable, and he leaned forward to study her, finding his nostrils suddenly filled with the warm, musky note of her perfume. He moved out of its seductive and dangerous range. 'What's the matter with you, Bella?' he asked softly. 'What's happened?'

Now was the time to tell him everything. But one look at the disquiet on his face, and the words stuck in her throat. 'Nothing has happened,' she floundered. 'Other than the fact I've left.'

'So you said.' He felt another flicker of irritation and made sure that it showed. 'But you still haven't come up with a good reason why—' A pause, while the black eyes bored into her. 'Mainly, I suspect, because you don't have one.' Normally, he wouldn't have been so rude to her—but then this was not a normal situation. 'So, Isabella,' he said silkily. 'I'm still waiting for some kind of explanation.'

Tell him. But, faced with the iron disapproval in the black eyes, she found that her nerve had crumbled again. 'I was bored.'

'You were bored.' He tapped the arm of his hair with a furious finger.

'OK, stressed then.'

'Stressed?' He looked at her with disbelief. 'What the hell has a beautiful young woman of twenty got to be stressed about? Is it a man?'

'No. There is no man.' And that *was* the truth.

'For God's sake, Bella—it isn't like you to be so fickle! I can't believe that an intelligent girl—*woman*—' he corrected immediately and a pulse began a slow, rhythmical dance at his temple, 'like you should throw everything away because you're "bored"! So what? Stick it out for a few months more—because believe me, *querida*,' he added grimly, 'There's nothing quite so "boring" as a dead-end job—which is all you'll get if you drop out of college!'

And suddenly she knew that she couldn't tell him. Not now. Not in ten minutes' time—maybe not ever. How could she risk the contempt which would follow as surely as night followed day? Not from Paulo, whom she'd adored as long as she could remember.

'I wasn't looking for your approval,' she said woodenly.

'You don't seem to be looking further than the end
of your nose!' he snapped. 'And just how are you planning to support yourself? Expecting Daddy to chip in, I
suppose?'

She glared at him. 'Of course not! I'll take whatever
I can get—I'm young and fit. I can cook. I'm good with
children. Fluent in English and Portuguese.'

'A very commendable CV,' he remarked drily.

'So you'd recommend me for a job, would you,
Paulo?'

'No, I damned well wouldn't!' His voice deepened
into a husky caress. 'But I would do everything in my
power to make you change your mind.' There was a
pause, and then he spoke to her with the ease and affection which had always existed between them, until temptation had reared its ugly head.

'Go home, Bella. Complete your studies. Come back
in a couple of years.' His eyes glittered as he imagined
what two years would do to her. 'And *then* I'll find a
job for you—on that I give you my word.'

She glanced down at her hands, unable to meet his
eyes as his voice gentled. In a couple of years her world
would have altered out of all recognition, in a way that
she still found utterly unimaginable. 'Yes, you're probably right,' she lied.

'So you'll go back to college?'

'I'll…think about it.' She made a pantomime of looking at her watch, affecting a look of surprise. 'Oh,
look—it's time I was going.'

'You're not going anywhere,' he protested. 'You've
only just arrived. Stay and see Eddie—he'll be back
soon.'

'No, I don't think I will.' She rose to her feet, anxious now to get away. Before he guessed. 'Maybe another day.'

'Where are you staying?'

'Just down the road,' she said evasively.

'Where?'

'At the Merton.'

'At the Merton,' he repeated thoughtfully.

He walked her to the front door just as they heard the sound of a key being slotted into the lock, and for some reason Paulo felt extraordinarily guilty as the door opened and there stood Judy—so cool and so blonde, wearing something soft and clinging in pale-blue cashmere, and a faint look of irritation on her face. Next to her stood his son, and the moment the boy saw Isabella his dark eyes lit up like lanterns.

'Bella!' he exclaimed, and immediately started speaking in Portuguese as he hurled himself into her arms. 'What are you doing here? Papa didn't tell me you were coming!'

'That's because Papa didn't know himself,' said Paulo, in the same language. 'Bella just turned up unannounced while you were out!'

'Are you coming to stay with us?' demanded Eddie. '*Please*, Bella! Please!'

'Eduardo, I can't,' answered Bella, her smile one of genuine regret. She had bonded with Eduardo from the word go—maybe because they had both had motherless childhoods. She had helped him with his riding and with his Portuguese and seen him grow from toddlerhood to a healthy young boy. And before very long, he would be towering above her as much as his father did. 'I'm going to be travelling around. I want to see as much of the country as I can.'

'Is this a private conversation,' asked the woman in blue, 'or can anyone join in?'

Paulo gave an apologetic smile and immediately switched to English. 'Judy! Forgive me! This is Isabella Fernandes. She's visiting England from Brazil. Isabella, this is Judy Jacob. She's—'

'I'm his girlfriend,' put in Judy helpfully.

Isabella prayed that her smile wouldn't crumple. 'Hello. It's nice to meet you.'

Paulo shot Judy a look which demanded co-operation. 'Isabella is a very old friend of the family—'

'Not *that* old,' corrected Judy softly, as she chose to ignore his silent request. 'In fact, she looks incredibly young to me.'

'Our fathers were at school together,' explained Paulo smoothly. 'And I've known Isabella all my life.'

'How very sweet.' Judy flashed a brief smile at Isabella and then leaned forward to plant a light kiss on Paulo's lips. 'Well, I hate to break the party up, sweetheart, but the show starts at—'

'And I really must go,' said Isabella hastily, because the sight of that proprietorial kiss was making her feel ill. 'Goodbye, Paulo. Goodbye, Judy—nice to have met you.' Her voice barely faltered over the insincere words. 'Goodbye, Eduardo.' She ruffled the boy's dark head and smiled down at him.

'But when will we see you?' Eduardo demanded.

'Oh, I'll be in touch,' she lied, but as she looked into the black glitter of Paulo's eyes she suspected that he knew as well as she did that she would not come back again. Because there was no place for her in his life here. No convenient slot she could fill—pregnant or otherwise. And if there had been the tiniest, most pathetic hope that she meant something more to him than just friendship… Well, that hope had been extinguished by a girlfriend who was the image of his late wife. A girlfriend who called him 'sweetheart' and who owned a key to his flat.

But then, what had she honestly expected? That she could turn up unannounced and tell him she'd run away from home—pregnant and alone—and that he would give that slow, lazy smile and solve all her problems for her?

She didn't stop for the traditional kissing of the cheeks—she didn't want to annoy Judy more than she already seemed to have done. Instead, she wrapped her coat tightly around her as she stepped out into the early evening and wondered just where she went from here.

CHAPTER TWO

'ISABELLA!' screamed a female voice from the bottom of the stairs. 'Can you get down here straight away?'

In her room at the top of the ugly, mock-Georgian house which stood in an 'upmarket estate', Isabella sighed. She was supposed to be off duty. Getting the rest which her body craved, and the doctor had demanded on her last visit to him. But that was easier said than done.

What did they want from her now, this noisy and dysfunctional family? she wondered tiredly. A pound of her flesh—would that be enough to keep them off her back for more than five minutes?

Wasn't it enough that she worked from dawn to dusk, looking after the lively twins who belonged to the Stafford family? Au pairs were supposed to *help* look after the children and engage in a little light housework, weren't they? And to have enough time for their own studies and recreation. They weren't supposed to cook and clean and iron and sew and babysit night after night for no extra money.

Sometimes Isabella found herself wondering just why she put up with treatment which clearly broke every employment law in the book. Was she weak? Or simply a fool?

But it didn't take long for her to realise exactly why she was willing to put up with such shoddy behaviour— one look in the mirror reassured her that she was not in any position to be choosy. The curve of her belly was as ripe as a watermelon about to burst, and Mrs Stafford—for all her faults—was the only prospective employer who'd agreed to take her baby on, as well.

Of course, there'd always been the option of going home to Brazil, or returning to the ranch. But how could she face her father like this?

When her furtively conducted pregnancy test had turned out to be positive, she'd been so stunned by disbelief that she hadn't felt strong enough to present her father with the unwelcome news.

And the longer she put off telling him—the more difficult the task had seemed. So that in the end it had seemed easier to run to England. To Paulo. Never dreaming that her life-long infatuation with the man would render her too proud to tell *him*, either.

Coming to the Staffords had seemed the only decision which made any sense at the time, but she'd lived to regret it since.

Or maybe the regret had something to do with letting down the two men who she knew adored her.

'Isa-*bella*!'

Resisting the urge to yell back at her boss to go away, Isabella levered herself off the bed and slipped her stockinged feet into a pair of comfortable slippers. If there was one thing she enjoyed about being pregnant—and so far it was the only thing she had enjoyed—it was allowing herself the freedom to dress purely for comfort. Elasticated waists and thick socks may have made her resemble an enormous sack of rice, but she felt too cumbersome to care.

'Coming!' she called, as she carefully made her way downstairs.

The twins came running out of the sitting room, their faces working with excitement. Charlie and Richie were seven year-old twins whose mission in life seemed to be to make their au pair's life as difficult as possible. But she'd grown fond of these two boys, with their big eyes and mischievous grins and excessively high energy levels.

Rosemary Stafford's methods of childcare had not been the ones Isabella would have chosen, but at least she was able to have a little influence on their lives.

She had tried to steer them away from the video games and television shows which had been their daily entertainment diet. At first, they'd protested loudly when she had insisted on sitting down and reading with them each evening, but they had grown to accept the ritual— even, she suspected, to secretly enjoy it.

'You've gotta vis'tor, Bella!' said Richie.

'Oh? Who is it?' asked Isabella.

'It's a *man*!'

Isabella blinked. Like who? 'But I don't know any men!' she protested.

Richie's mother appeared at the sitting room door. 'Well, that's a *bit* of an exaggeration, surely!' she said in a low voice, looking pointedly at Isabella's swollen belly. 'You must have known at least one.'

Isabella refused to rise to the remark—but then she'd had a lot of practice at ignoring her boss's barbed comments.

Ever since she'd first moved in, Rosemary Stafford had made constant references to Isabella's pregnant and unmarried state, slipping easily into the role of some kind of moral guardian.

Isabella thought this was rather surprising, considering that Mrs Stafford had become pregnant with the twins while her husband was still living with his first wife!

She gave a thin smile. 'Who is it?'

Mrs. Stafford was trying hard not to look impressed. 'He *says* he's a friend of the family.'

She could see Charlie and Richie staring up at her, but Isabella's smile didn't slip. Even though a thousand warning notes were playing a symphony in her subconscious. 'Did he give his name?'

'He did.'

'And?'

'It's Paulo somebody-or-other.'

Isabella's mouth froze. 'Paulo D-Dantas?' she managed.

'That's the one,' said Mrs Stafford briskly. 'He's in the drawing room. You'd better come along and speak to him—he doesn't seem like the kind of man who likes to be kept waiting.'

Isabella's hand strayed anxiously to her hair. What was he doing here? And what must she look like? Her eyes flickered over to where the hall mirror told its own story.

Her thick dark-brown hair had been carelessly heaped on top of her head, secured by a tortoiseshell comb. Her face was pale, thanks to the English winter—a pallor made more intense by the fact that she wasn't wearing a scrap of make-up.

'Why on earth didn't you tell me?' hissed Mrs Stafford.

'Tell you what?'

'That a man like *that* was the father of your child?'

Isabella opened her mouth to protest, but by then her employer was throwing open the door to the sitting room and it was too late to do anything other than go in and face the music.

The room seemed darker than usual and Isabella wondered why, until she saw that Paulo was standing staring out of the window and seemed to be blocking out much of the light.

He turned slowly as she came into the room and she saw his relaxed pose stiffen into one of complete disbelief as he took in her physical condition. The exaggerated bulge of her stomach. The heavy weight of her breasts.

She saw his black eyes glitter as they hovered on the unfamiliar swell, and she tried to read what was written in them. Shock. Horror. Disdain. Yes, all of those. And she found herself wishing that she could turn around and run out of the room again or, better still, turn back the clock completely. Something—anything—other than have to face that bitter look in this sorry and vulnerable state.

'Isabella.' He inclined his head in formal greeting, but the low-pitched voice sounded oddly flat.

He was wearing a dark suit—as if he had come straight from some high-powered business meeting without bothering to change first. The sleekly cut trousers made the most of lean, long legs and the double-breasted jacket hugged the broad shoulders and chest. Against the brilliant whiteness of his shirt, his skin gleamed softly olive. She had never seen him so formally dressed before, and the conventional clothes seemed to add to the distance between them.

Isabella felt the first flutterings of apprehension.

'Hello, Paulo,' she said steadily. 'You should have warned me you were coming.'

'And if I had?' His voice was deadly soft. 'Would you still have received me like this?'

She saw from the dark stare which lanced through her like a laser that it was not a rhetorical question. 'No. Probably not,' she admitted.

Mrs Stafford, who had been gazing up at Paulo like a star-struck schoolgirl, now turned to Isabella with a look of reprimand. 'Isabella—where are your manners? Aren't you going to introduce me to your friend?' She gave Paulo the benefit of a sickly smile.

Isabella swallowed. 'Paulo, this is Rosemary Stafford—my boss. Paulo is—'

'Very welcome,' purred Mrs Stafford. 'Very welcome indeed. Perhaps we can offer you a little refreshment after your journey? Isabella, why don't you go and make Mr Dantas a drink?'

Paulo said, in Portuguese. 'Get rid of her.'

Isabella felt inexplicably nervous. And certainly not up to defying him. 'I wonder if you'd mind leaving us, Mrs Stafford? It's just that I'd like to talk to my…friend—' she hesitated over a word which did not seem appropriate '—in private.'

Rosemary Stafford's pretty, painted mouth became a petulant-looking pout. 'Yes, I expect you do. I expect you have many issues to resolve,' she said, with stiff emphasis, and swept out of the sitting room, past where Charlie and Richie were hovering by the door, trying to listen to the conversation inside.

Paulo walked over to the door and gave the boys a slight, almost apologetic shrug of his shoulders, before quietly closing the door on them. And when he turned to face Isabella—she almost recoiled from the look of fury which burned from his eyes.

As though she were some insect he had just found squashed beneath his heel and he wished she would crawl right back where she had come from. But what right did he have to judge her? She thought of all she'd endured since arriving in England, and suddenly Paulo's anger seemed little to bear, in comparison. She drew her shoulders back to meet his gaze without flinching.

'You'd better start explaining,' he said flatly.

'I owe you no explanation.'

A pulse began a slow beat in his temple. 'You don't think so?' he said quietly.

'My pregnancy has nothing whatsoever to do with you, Paulo.'

He gave a hollow, bitter laugh. 'Maybe in the conventional sense it doesn't—but you involved me the moment you told your father that you were going to pay me a visit.'

She screwed her eyes up and stared at him in confusion. 'But that was months ago! Before I left Brazil. And I did visit you. Remember? That day I came to see you in your flat?'

'Oh, I most certainly do,' he said, grimly resurrecting the memory he had spent months trying to forget. 'I wondered then why you seemed so anxious. So jumpy.' He had been intensely aroused by her that day, and had thought that the feeling was mutual—it had seemed the only rational explanation for the incredible tension between them. But he wasn't going to tell her that. Not now. 'I also sensed that you were holding back—something you weren't telling me. And so you were.' He shook his head. 'My God!' he said slowly.

'And now you know!'

'Yes, now I know,' he agreed acidly. 'I put your tiredness down to jet-lag—when all the time...' He looked down over at her swollen stomach with renewed amazement. 'All the time you were pregnant. Pregnant! Carrying a *baby*.' The word came out on a breath of disbelief. 'How can this have happened, Bella?'

She met his accusing gaze and then she *did* flinch. 'Do you really want me to answer that?'

'No. You're right. I don't!' He sucked in a hot, angry breath. 'Don't you realise that your father is worried *sick* about you?'

'How can you know that?'

'Because he rang me yesterday from Brazil.'

'W-why should he ring *you*?' she stumbled in confusion.

'Think about it,' he grated. 'He asked me to come and see you, to find out what the problem is. Why your letters have been so vague, your phone-calls so infrequent.' He shook his head and the black eyes lanced through her with withering contempt. 'I certainly don't relish telling him the reason why.'

'So he still doesn't know?' she questioned urgently. 'About the baby?'

'It would seem not,' he answered coldly. 'Unless he's a very good actor indeed. His main anxiety seemed to stem from the fact that he could not understand why you had chosen to flunk university to become an au pair.'

'But he knew all that! I wrote to him—and told him that living in England was an education in itself!' she protested.

She'd kept her father supplied with regular and fairly chatty letters—though carefully omitting to mention her momentous piece of news. As far as he knew, she would probably go back and repeat her final year at college. She hadn't mentioned when she was going home and he hadn't asked. And she thought that she'd convinced him that she was sophisticated enough to want to see the world. 'I've been writing to him every single week!'

The chill did not leave his voice. 'So he said. But unfortunately letters sent from abroad are read and re-

read and scoured for hidden meanings. Your father suspected that you were not happy, though he couldn't put his finger on why that was. He asked me to come to see whether all was well.' Another cold, hollow laugh. 'And here I am.'

'You needn't have bothered!'

'No, you're right. I needn't.' His mouth curved with disdain as he gazed around the bland room, with its unadorned walls and rows of videos where there should have been books. Littered on the thick, cream carpet were empty chocolate wrappers. 'My, my, my—this is certainly some *classy* hide-out you've chosen, Isabella!' he drawled sarcastically.

His criticism was valid, but no less infuriating because of that. She struggled to find something positive to say about it. 'I like the boys,' she came up with finally. 'I've grown very fond of them.'

'You mean the two hooligans who nearly rode their skateboards straight into the path of my car?'

Isabella went white. 'But they aren't supposed to play with them in the road!' How was she supposed to watch them twenty-four hours a day? 'They *know* that!'

Paulo narrowed his eyes as he took a look at her pale, thin face, which seemed so at odds with her bloated body and felt adrenaline rush to fire his blood. He'd felt a powerful sense of injustice once before in his life, when his wife had died, but the feeling which enveloped him now came a pretty close second.

And this time he was not powerless to act.

'Answer me one question,' he commanded.

Isabella shook her head. This one she'd been anticipating. 'I'm not telling you the name of the baby's father, if that's your question.'

'It's not.' He almost smiled. Almost. He had somehow

known that she would proudly deny him that. But he was glad. Knowledge could be a dangerous thing—and if he knew, then he might just be tempted to find the bastard responsible, and to…to… 'Is there anything special keeping you in this house, this particular area?'

'Not really. Just…the twins.'

Which told him more than she probably intended. That the father of her baby did not live locally. Nor live in this house. It wasn't probable—but it was possible. His mouth tightened. Thank God. 'Then go upstairs and get your things together,' he ordered curtly. 'We're going.'

It was one more bizarre experience in a long line of bizarre experiences. She stared at him blankly. 'Going where?'

'Anywhere,' he gritted. 'Just so long as it's out of here!'

Automatically, Isabella shook her head, as practical difficulties momentarily obscured the fact that he was being so high-handed with her. 'I can't leave—'

'Oh, yes, you can!'

'But the boys need me!'

'Maybe they do,' he agreed. 'But your baby needs you more. And right at this moment you look as if you could do with a decent meal and a good night's sleep!' He steadied his breath with difficulty. 'So just go and get your things together.'

'I'm not going anywhere!' she said, with a stubbornness which smacked of raging hormones.

Paulo gave a faint, regretful smile. He had hoped that it would not come to this, but he could be as ruthless as the next man when he believed in what he was fighting for. 'I'm afraid that you are,' he disagreed grimly.

Suddenly she wondered why she was tolerating that

clipped, flat command. She lifted her chin in a defiant thrust. 'You can't *make* me, Paulo!'

'I agree that it might not be wise to be seen carrying a heavily pregnant woman out to my car—though I am quite prepared to, if that's what it takes,' he told her, a soft threat underpinning his words. 'You can fight me every inch of the way if you want, Isabella, but I hope it won't come to that. Because whatever happens, I will win. I always do.'

'And if I refuse?'

Her eyes asked him a question, a question he had no desire to answer—but maybe it was the only way to make her see that he was deadly serious.

'Then I could threaten to tell your father the truth about why you left Brazil. But the truth might set in motion all kinds of repercussions which you may prefer not to have to deal with at the moment. Am I right?'

'You wouldn't do that?' she breathed.

'Oh, yes. Be assured that I would!'

She stared back at him with helpless rage. 'Bastard!' she hissed.

'Please do not use that particular term as an insult!' he snapped. 'It is entirely inappropriate, given your current condition.' His eyes flickered coldly over her bare fingers. 'Unless you have an undisclosed wedding to add to your list of secrets?' He read her answer in the proud tremble of her lips. 'No? Well, then my dear Isabella— that leaves you little option other than to come away with me, doesn't it?'

It was far too easy. Far too tempting. But what use would it serve? Could she bear to grow used to that cold judgement which had hardened his face so that he didn't look like Paulo any more, but some dark and disapproving stranger? 'I can't just leave without notice! What will the boys do?'

He refrained from telling her that her priorities were in shockingly bad order. 'They have their mother, don't they? And she will just have to look after them for a change. Does she work?'

Isabella shook her head. 'Not outside the home,' she answered automatically, as her employer had taught her to. In fact, Mrs Stafford had made leisure into an Olympic sport. She shopped. She had coffee. She lunched. And very occasionally she lay in bed all day, making telephone calls to her friends...

'Run upstairs—'

She turned on him then, moving her bulky body awkwardly as the emotion of having borne her secret alone for so long finally took its toll. She blinked back the tears which welled up saltily in her eyes. 'I can't run anywhere at the moment!' She swallowed.

He resisted the urge to draw her into his arms and to give her the physical comfort he suspected that she badly needed. It was not his place to give it. Not now and certainly not here. 'I know you can't—that's why I'm offering to help you. If you go and pack, I will deal with your employer for you.'

'Shouldn't I tell her myself?'

He thought how naive and innocent she could look and sound—despite the very physical evidence to the contrary. He shook his head impatiently. 'She's going to be angry, isn't she?'

Isabella pushed a dark strand of hair away from her face with the back of her hand. 'Furious.'

'Well, then—you can do without her fury. Let her take it out on me instead. Go on, *querida*. Go now.'

The familiar word made her heart clench and she had

to put her hand onto the back of a chair to steady herself. She had not heard her mother-tongue spoken for months, and it penetrated a chink in the protective armour she had attempted to build around herself. She nodded, then did as he asked, lumbering up to her room at the top of the house with as much speed as she could manage.

She did not have many things to pack. She'd brought few clothes with her to England, and what few she had no longer fitted her. Instead, she'd bought garments which were suitable for this cold, new climate and the ungainly new shape of her body.

Big, sloppy jumpers, two dresses and a couple of pairs of trousers with huge, elasticated waists which she was currently stretching to just about as far as they could go.

She had been forced to buy new underwear, too—and had felt like an outcast in the shop. As if everyone knew she was all alone with her pregnancy. And that no man would ever feast his eyes with love and pride on the huge, pendulous breasts which strained against the functional bra she'd been forced to purchase.

She swept the clothes and her few toiletries into the suitcase and located her passport. On the windowsill stood a wedding-day photo of her parents and, with a heavy heart, she added it to the rest of her possessions.

And then, with a final glance round at the box-room which had been her home for the last five months, she quietly shut the door behind her.

At the foot of the stairs, a deputation was awaiting her. Towering over the small group was Paulo, his hair as black as ebony, when viewed from above. Next to him stood Rosemary Stafford, her fury almost palpable as she attempted to control the two boys.

'Will you keep *still*?' she was yelling, but they were taking no notice of her.

Charlie and Richie were buzzing around the hallway like demented flies—whipped up by the unexpected excitement of what was happening, and yet looking vaguely uncertain. As if they could anticipate that changes would shortly be made to their young lives. And correctly guessing that they would not like those changes at all.

Isabella reached the bottom of the stairs and Paulo took the suitcase from her hand. 'I'll put this in the car for you.'

She felt like calling after him, Please don't leave me! but that *would* be weak and cowardly. Instead, she turned to Rosemary Stafford and forced herself to remember just how many times she had helped the older woman out. All the occasions when she had agreed to babysit with little more than a moment's notice. And never complained. Not once. 'I'm sorry to have to leave so suddenly—'

'Oh, spare me your lies!' hissed Rosemary Stafford venomously.

'But they're *not* lies!' Isabella protested. 'It isn't practical to carry on like this. Honestly. The truth is that I *have* been getting awfully tired—'

'Oh? And what about other, earlier so-called "truths"?' Rosemary Stafford's glossy pink lips gaped uglily. 'Like your assurance that the father of your baby wasn't going to turn up out of the blue and start creating havoc with my routine?'

Isabella was about to explain that Paulo was not the father of her baby—but what was the point? What could she say? The boys were standing there, wide-eyed and listening to every word. Trying to make two seven-year-old boys understand the reality of the whole bizarre situation was more than she felt prepared to take on right then.

Instead, she reached out an unsteady hand and ruffled Richie's blond hair. Of the two boys, he'd been the one who had crept the furthest into her heart, and she didn't want to hurt him. 'I'll write,' she began uncertainly.

'Take your hands away from him, and don't be so *stupid*!' spat out Mrs Stafford. 'What will you write to a seven-year-old boy about? The birth? Or the *conception*?'

Isabella shuddered, wondering how Mrs Stafford could possibly say things like that in front of her children.

'It's time to leave, Isabella,' came a low voice from behind them, and Isabella turned to see Paulo framed in the neo-Georgian doorway. His face was shadowed, the features so still that they might have been carved from some rare, pitch-dark marble. Only the eyes glittered— hard and black and icy-cold.

She wondered how long he had been standing there, listening, whether he had heard Mrs Stafford's assumption that he was the father of her baby.

And her own refusal to deny it.

'Isabella,' prompted Paulo softly. 'Come.'

Impulsively she bent and briefly put her arms round both boys. Richie was crying, and it took every bit of Isabella's willpower not to join in with his tears, knowing that it would be self-indulgent to break down and confuse them even more. Instead, she contented herself with a swift and fierce kiss on the top of each sweet, blond head.

'I *will* write!' she reaffirmed in an urgent whisper, as Paulo took her elbow like an invalid, and guided her out to the car.

CHAPTER THREE

As soon as the front door had shut behind them, Paulo let go of Isabella's elbow and she found herself missing its warmth and support immediately.

'The car is a little way up the street,' he said, still in that same flat tone which she'd never heard him use before.

He'd parked it there deliberately. Just in case. He had not known what he expected to find. Or who. He hadn't known if she would come willingly. And how he would've coped, had she refused. Because some instinct had told him even then, that he would not be leaving without her.

Isabella walked beside him towards the car, suspecting that he'd slowed his normal pace down in order for her to keep pace with him. She got out of breath so easily these days. 'Where are you taking me?'

'Taking implies force,' he corrected, looking down at her dark head, which only reached up to his shoulder. She seemed much too tiny to be bursting ripe with pregnancy. 'And you seem to be accompanying me willingly enough.'

What woman wouldn't? she thought, with another wistful pang. 'Where?' she repeated huskily.

A plane droned overhead, and he briefly lifted his face to stare at it. 'For now, you will have to come home with me—' He sent her a searing glance as if he anticipated her objection. 'Think about it before you say anything, Bella. It makes the most sense.'

If anything could be said to make sense at that precise moment, then yes, she supposed that it did. And hadn't that been her first choice? Before she'd seen him prowling half-naked around his own territory—like some sleek and beautiful cat? *Gato.* Before she'd seen the beautiful woman who'd frozen her out so effectively. Before she'd decided that she could not face him with her terrible secret.

'Doesn't it?'

Isabella nodded, wondering what Judy was going to say *this* time. 'I suppose so.'

'As to what happens after that...' A silky pause. 'There are a number of options open to you.'

'I'm not going back to Brazil!' she declared quietly. 'And you can't make me!'

He let that one go. For the moment. 'Here's my car.'

A midnight-blue sports car was parked with precision close to the kerb, and Isabella stared at the low, gleaming bodywork in dismay.

'What's the matter?'

She glanced up to find that the black eyes were fixed intently on her face. He must have noticed her hesitation. She gestured to her stomach, placing her hands on either side of her bump, to draw his attention to it. 'Look—'

'I'm looking,' he replied, taken aback by the sudden hurl of his heart as one of her hands strayed dangerously close to the heavy swell of her breast.

'I'm so big and so bulky, and your car is so stream-lined.'

He held the door open for her. 'You think you won't fit?'

'Look away,' she said. 'It won't be a graceful sight.'

She began to ease her legs inside and his face grew grim as he turned back to look at the house they had just left—where two small boys forlornly watched them from an upstairs window. He did not know what lay ahead, beyond offering her temporary refuge, but already he suspected that his loyalties might be torn. How could they not be?

He'd known Isabella's father for years—ever since he was a boy himself. And for the last ten summers since his wife's death had accepted Luis's hospitality for both himself and his son.

Eddie had been just a baby when his mother had died so needlessly and so tragically in a hit-and-run accident that had produced national revulsion, but no conviction. The man—or woman—who had killed Elizabeth remained free to this day. In the lonely and insecure days following her death, it had seemed vital to Paulo that Eddie should know something of his South American roots.

As a father himself, Paulo felt duty-bound to inform Luis Fernandes what was happening to his daughter. But Isabella was not a child. Far from it. Would she expect him to collude with *her*? To keep quiet about the baby? And for how long?

He waited until they'd eased away from the kerb, before jerking his head back in the direction of the house.

'How long were you planning to stay there?'

'I don't know.' She stared at the road ahead. 'I just took it day by day. Mrs Stafford said that I could work the baby into my routine.'

Paulo's long fingers dug into the steering wheel. 'But you must have *some* idea, Isabella! Until the baby was...what...how old? Six months? A year? Would you then have returned to Brazil with a grandchild for your father to see? Or were you planning to keep it hidden from him forever?'

'I told you,' she answered tiredly, wishing that he wouldn't keep asking her these questions—though she noted that he'd refrained from asking the most fundamental question of all. 'I honestly *don't know*. And not because I hadn't thought about it, either. Believe me, I'd thought about it so much that the thoughts seemed to just go round and round inside my head, until sometimes I felt like I would burst—'

Paulo's mouth hardened. Hadn't he felt exactly like that after Elizabeth's death? When the world seemed to make no sense at all? He stole a glance at her strained, white face and felt an unwilling surge of compassion. 'But the more you thought about it, the more confused you got—so that you were still no closer to deciding what to do? Is that right?'

His perception disarmed her, just as the warmth and comfort of the car soothed her more than she'd expected to be soothed. Isabella felt her mouth begin to tremble, and she turned to look out of the window at the city speeding by, so that he wouldn't see. 'Yes. How could I be?' She kept her voice low. 'Because whatever decision I reach—is bound to hurt someone, somewhere.'

Her words were so quiet that he could barely hear, but Paulo could sense that she was close to tears. A deep vein of disquiet ran through him. Now was not the time to fire questions at her—not when she looked so little and pale and vulnerable.

He thought how spare the flesh looked on her bones— all her old voluptuousness gone. As if, despite the absurdly swollen bump of her pregnancy, a puff of wind could blow her away.

'You haven't been eating properly,' he accused.

'There isn't a lot of room for food these days.'

'Have you had supper?'

'Well, no,' she admitted. She'd been seeking refuge in her room: too tired to bother going downstairs to hunt through the junk food in the Staffords' fridge for something which looked vaguely nutritional.

'Your baby needs sustenance,' he growled. 'And so, for that matter, do you. I'm taking you for something to eat.'

Nausea welled up in her throat. She shook her head. 'I can't face the thought of food at the moment. Too much has happened—surely you can understand that?'

'You can try.' His mouth twisted into a mocking smile. 'For me.'

She knotted her fingers together in her lap. 'I suppose I'm not going to get any peace unless I agree?'

'No, you're not,' he agreed. 'Just console yourself with the thought that I'm doing it for your own good.'

'You're so kind, Paulo.'

He heard the tentative attempt at sarcasm and oddly enough it made him smile. At least her spirit hadn't been entirely extinguished. 'More practical than kind,' he murmured. 'We need to talk and you need to decide your future. And we can't do that in private at my house.'

'Because of Eduardo?'

'That's right.' He wondered how he could possibly explain away her pregnancy to the son who idolised the ground she walked on. 'He'll be curious to know why you're here—and we can't give him any answers if we don't know what they are ourselves. And it might just come as a shock for him to see you so—' the words tasted bitter on his lips '—so heavily pregnant.'

She remembered the cool, blonde beauty who had let herself in and forced herself to ask the question. 'What about Judy? Won't she mind me landing myself on you?'

'I shouldn't think so.'

There was an odd kind of pause and she turned her head to stare at the darkened profile.

'I'm not seeing her any more,' he said.

'Oh.' Isabella was unprepared for the sudden warm rush of relief, but she tried not to let it show in her voice. 'Oh, dear. What happened?'

Paulo compressed his lips, resisting the urge to tell her that it was none of her business. Because it was. Because somehow—unknowingly and unwittingly—Isabella had exposed him to doubts about his relationship with Judy which had led to its eventual demise.

He'd thought that shared interests and a mutually satisfactory sex-life were all that he needed from a relationship. But Isabella's visit had made him aware that there was no real *spark* between him and Judy. And something which he'd thought suited him suddenly seemed like an awful waste of time. 'We kind of drifted apart,' he said.

'But you're still friends?'

'I suppose so,' he answered reluctantly. Because that was what Judy had wanted. She'd settled for 'friendship' once she realised he'd meant it when he told her it was over. But he knew deep down that they could never be true friends—she still wanted him too badly for that. 'We're not supposed to be discussing *my* love-life, Isabella.'

'Well, I don't want to discuss mine,' she said quietly.

'Does that mean you aren't going to tell who who the father of your baby is?'

Isabella flinched. 'That's right.'

'Do I know him?'

'What makes you think I would tell you, if even you did?'

He found her misplaced loyalty both exasperating and admirable. 'And what if I made you tell me?' he challenged.

The streetlights flickered strange shadows over his face and Isabella felt suddenly uncertain. 'You couldn't.'

'Want to bet?'

'I n-never bet.'

'I'm not sure that I believe you,' he said softly. 'When you are living, walking proof that you took a *huge* gamble.' And lost, he thought—though he didn't say it. The look on her face told him he didn't have to. The car came to stop at some traffic lights and he shifted in his seat to get a better look at her.

And Isabella forgot the baby. Forgot everything. Through the dim light, all she could see in that moment were his eyes. Dark, like chocolate, and rich like chocolate, and sexy like chocolate. And chocolate was what Isabella had been craving for the past eight months. 'Paulo—'

But he'd turned his attention back to the road ahead. 'We're here,' he said grimly.

She heaved a sigh of relief as he pulled up outside an Italian pasta bar. Heaven only knew what she'd been about to blurt out when she had whispered his name like that. At least the activity of eating might distract him from his interrogation—and maybe she was hungrier than she had previously thought. It would certainly make a change to have a meal cooked for her.

The restaurant was small and lit by candles, and almost full—and Isabella was certain that they would be turned away. But no. It seemed that here they knew him well. Paulo asked for, and got, a table in one of the recesses of the room—well away from the other customers.

She glanced down at the menu she'd been given, at the meaningless swirl of words there. And when she looked up again, it was to find him studying her intently.

'Do you know what you want?'

She shook her head. 'No.'

He jabbed a finger halfway down his menu. 'Why don't you try some spinach lasagne?' he suggested. 'Lots of nutrients to build you up. And you, *querida*, could certainly do with some building up.'

She nodded obediently. 'All right.'

He wasn't used to such passivity—not from Isabella—and thought how wan her face looked as the waiter came over to their table. 'Drink some tomato juice,' he instructed, almost roughly. 'You like that, don't you?'

'Thanks. I will.' She shook out her napkin and smoothed it out carefully on her lap as he gave their order.

'So.' He traced a thoughtful finger on the crisp, white cloth and leaned across the table towards her. 'We—or rather *you*—have a few big decisions to make.'

'I'm not going home!

'No. So you said.' His mouth hardened. 'Anyway, your objection is academic, isn't it, Bella? No airline will allow you to fly in such an advanced stage of pregnancy.' He paused, his dark gaze on her belly, as if he could estimate the gestation just by looking. 'And you're...how many weeks?'

She hesitated. 'Thirty-seven.'

'Only three weeks to go,' he observed, his eyes burning into her. 'So when did you conceive?'

Isabella blushed. 'I don't have to answer that.'

'No, you don't,' he agreed. 'But I can work it out for myself in any case.' His eyes shuttered to dark slits as he did a few rapid sums in his head, then flickered open to stare at her with astonishment. 'That takes us back to just around Carnival time.'

'Paulo, *must* you?'

He ignored her objection, still frowning. 'That means you must have become pregnant just after I left.'

She supposed that there was no point in denying it. 'Yes.'

'Or maybe it was *during* my visit?' he suggested, unprepared for the lightning-bolt of jealousy.

'No!' she shot back.

He frowned again, not seeming to care that the waiter was depositing their food and wine before them. 'So who is it? I don't remember seeing you with anyone. No ardent lover hanging around the place. I don't remember you rushing off every minute to be with someone.'

Quite the opposite, in fact. She had been at *his* side most minutes of the day. Her father had even made a joke about it. *She has become your little shadow, Paulo,* the older man had laughed and Isabella had aimed a mock-punch at her father's stomach while Paulo had watched the movement of her lush breasts with hungry eyes and a guilty heart. And been very sure that if his host knew what was going on in his mind, then he would have kicked him off the ranch there and then.

'So who is it?' he asked again, only this time his voice sounded brittle.

Isabella mechanically ate a mouthful of pasta, forcing herself to meet his eyes. 'Is my coming to stay with you conditional on me telling you who the father is?'

'I don't need to know his name. I'm certainly not going to try to wring it out of you.' There was a long and dangerous pause. 'But if he turns up, demanding to see you—'

'He won't,' she put in hurriedly. 'It won't happen. I give you my word, Paulo.'

'You sound very sure,' he observed. He looked over the rim of his wineglass, fixing her with a dark gaze which was as intense as his next soft question. 'Does that mean that the affair is definitely over?'

The *affair*? If only he knew! 'Yes.' Isabella swallowed. She owed him the truth. Or as much of the truth as she dared give without earning making herself sound like the biggest fool who ever walked the earth. 'It's over. It never really got off the ground, if you must know.' Her eyes glittered with a defiant kind of pride as she stared at the man she had idolised for as long as she could remember.

'But I can't come to stay with you, not even for a minute—not if you despise me for what I've done, Paulo.'

'Despise you?' He looked across the table, saw the stubborn little tilt of her chin, and felt a wave of anger wash over him. What a way to have a first baby, he thought bitterly. It shouldn't be like this—not for any woman—but especially not for Isabella.

He remembered Eduardo's impending arrival, when Elizabeth had planned everything right down to the very last detail. Nothing had been left to chance, save chance itself. He had joked that her hospital bag had been packed almost from the moment of conception, and Elizabeth had laughed, too. His voice softened. 'Why on earth would I despise you?'

'Why do you think?' Isabella stared down at her plate with eyes which were suddenly bright. 'Because I'm going to have a baby. I'm going to be an unmarried mother! I've let my father down,' she husked. 'And myself!'

He leaned further across the table towards her, so that the flame of the candle was reflected in the black eyes. 'Now listen to me, Isabella Fernandes, and stop beating yourself up!' he whispered fiercely. 'We aren't living in the Dark Ages. You'll be bringing a baby up on your own—so what? A third of the population in England is *divorced*, for God's sake—and there are countless children who are the casualties of broken marriages. At least your child won't have to witness the deterioration of a relationship.'

'But I didn't *want* to have a baby like this!'

'I know you didn't.' He took her hand in his, staring down at it as it lay inertly in his palm. It felt small and cold and lifeless and he began to massage the palm with the pad of his thumb, stroking some kind of warmth back into it. He felt her trembling response and found himself filled with a sudden fierce need to comfort her. Protect her.

'There is no Merton Hotel, is there?' he asked suddenly.

She glanced up. 'How do you know that?'

His mouth twisted into a strange kind of smile. 'How do you think? I came looking for you.'

'*Did* you?'

'Sure I did.'

After she'd left his house so abruptly, he'd gone to the theatre with Judy. He had sat through the show feeling distracted and bored and had been forced to endure all kinds of intrusive questions afterwards at supper, when Judy had been determined to find out everything she could about Isabella.

Too much wine had made Judy tearful and very slightly hysterical as she'd accused him of concealing something about his relationship with the Brazilian girl.

She'd made accusations about Isabella which had appalled him nearly as much as they had aroused him...

Grim-faced, he'd driven her home and resisted all her attempts to seduce him. Afterwards, he had gone home and phoned Directory Enquiries for the number of the Merton Hotel, only to discover that no such place existed.

So Isabella had not wanted him to find her, he remembered thinking, with faint surprise, because women usually made it easy for him to contact them—not the opposite. But that, he had decided reluctantly, was her prerogative.

And now he knew why.

He stared at her. 'Just why *did* you come to see me that day, Bella?' he asked. 'Was it to ask for my help?'

She hesitated. 'I... Yes. Yes, it was.'

'But something changed your mind. I wonder what it was.' His eyes narrowed with interest. 'Why did you go away without telling me?'

'I couldn't go through with it. When it came down to it, I just couldn't face telling you.'

'And that's it?' he demanded.

Again, she hesitated, but she knew she couldn't admit that she'd been intimidated by his girlfriend. And by the very fact that he had one. 'That's it.' She turned her face up to his and stumbled out his name. 'Oh, Paulo!' she sighed. 'Whatever have I *done*?'

The choked little words stabbed at him, and he gave her hand one final squeeze. 'There's nothing you can do about it. You've been unlucky, that's all—'

'No, please don't say that.' She kept her voice low. 'This is a baby we're talking about! Not a piece of bad luck!'

'That's not what I meant. You took a risk—and

you've paid the ultimate price for that risk.' He gave a bitter laugh. 'Didn't anyone ever tell you, Bella, that there's no such thing as safe sex?'

But he found that his words produced unwanted images—images of Isabella being intimate with another man, her dark hair spread in a shining fan across a stranger's pillow and a bitter taste began to taint his mouth. He put his napkin down on the table and threw her a look of dark challenge. 'I just hope it was worth it, *querida*.'

Worth it? Isabella stared down at her plate, but all she could see was a blur of tears. If only he knew, she thought. If only he knew.

CHAPTER FOUR

IT WAS getting on for nine o'clock when Paulo drew up in the quiet, tree-lined crescent. It was a cold, clear night and moonlight washed over the tall town houses, making them silvery-pale and ghost-like.

'Will Eduardo be asleep?' whispered Isabella, sleepy herself after the meal which she had surprised herself—and him—by almost finishing.

'You obviously have idealistic views on children's bedtime,' he answered drily as he put his key in the lock. 'He'll be playing on his computer, I imagine.' He opened the front door and ushered her inside, dumping Isabella's bag on the floor just inside the hall. 'Hello!' he called softly.

There was the sound of dishes being stacked some-where, and then a woman of about fifty appeared, wiping her damp hands down the sides of her trousers. She had short, curly red hair which was flecked with grey and a freckled face which was completely bare of make-up. Her navy trousers and navy polo-shirt were so neat and well-pressed that they looked like a uniform. She gave Isabella's suitcase a brief, curious look before smiling at Paulo.

'Ah, good! You're back just in time to read your son a story!'

'But he says he's too old for stories,' objected Paulo, with a smile.

'Yes, I know he does—unless his Papa is telling them. You're the exception who proves the rule, Paulo! As always.' Her gaze moved back to Isabella and she gave her a friendly smile. 'Hello!'

'Jessie, I'd like you to meet Isabella Fernandes—who is a very old family friend.'

'Yes, I know—Eddie's talked about you a lot,' said Jessie, still smiling.

'And, Isabella—this is Jessie Taylor, who's so much more than a housekeeper! How would you describe yourself Jessie?'

'As your willing slave, Paulo, how else? Nice to meet you, Isabella.' Jessie held her hand out. 'Your father owns that amazing cattle ranch, doesn't he?'

'The very same.' Isabella nodded.

'Don't you miss Brazil terribly?'

'Only in the winter!' Isabella pulled her raincoat closer and gave a mock-shiver, grateful for Jessie's tact in not drawing attention to the baby.

'Isabella is going to be staying here with us for the time being,' said Paulo.

'Oh. Right.' Jessie nodded. 'That's in the spare room, is it?' she questioned delicately.

Paulo's eyes narrowed. Did Jessie honestly think that he'd brought a woman back here in the latter stages of her pregnancy for nights of mad, passionate sex?

He stared at Isabella's pink cheeks and guessed that she'd picked up on it, too.

'Yes, of course,' he said deliberately. 'In the spare room. Is the bed made up?'

'No,' said Jessie briskly. 'But I can do that now, before I go.'

'Oh, please don't worry,' said Isabella quickly. 'I'm not helpless—I can do it myself. Really!'

But Jessie shook her head. 'Good heavens, no—I

wouldn't dream of letting you! You look dead on your feet. Why don't you sit down, my dear?'

Isabella hesitated.

'Go on, sit down,' ordered Paulo softly. 'Make yourself at home.'

She was too tired to argue with him, thinking how easy and how pleasurable it was to have Paulo make the decisions.

She sank down onto one of the two vast sofas which dominated the room, and gingerly removed the shoes from her swollen feet. She glanced up to find him watching her, his brow criss-crossed with little lines of concern, and she produced a faint smile. 'You did tell me to make myself at home.'

'So I did. I guess I was just expecting you to argue back,' he observed drily. 'I had no idea you could be *quite* so stubborn.'

'And I had no idea you could be *quite* so domineering!'

'Didn't you?' he mocked softly and, when she didn't answer, he smiled. 'Stay there—I'm going in to say goodnight to Eddie.'

He found his son tucked up underneath the duvet, his eyes heavy with sleep.

'Hello, Papa,' Eddie yawned.

'Hello, son,' smiled Paulo softly. 'Did you get my note?'

'Uh-huh.' Eddie jammed a fist in his eye and rubbed it, giving another yawn. 'How's Bella?'

'She's…tired. And she's going to be staying with us.'

The child's face lit up. '*Is* she? That's fantastic! How long for?'

'I don't know yet.' Paulo paused as he tried to work out how to explain the complications of a very adult situation to a ten-year-old. But children dealt with simple truth best. 'She's going to have a baby, you see.'

Eddie removed the fist and blinked up at his father. 'Wow! When?'

Paulo smiled. 'Soon. Very soon.'

Eddie sat bolt upright in bed. 'And will the baby come and live here, too?'

'I doubt it,' said Paulo gently. 'They'll probably go back home to Brazil once it's been born.'

'Oh,' said Eddie disappointedly, and snuggled back down under the duvet. 'Judy rang.'

'Did she?' Paulo frowned. He had always been completely straight with the women in his life. From the start he told them that he wasn't looking for love, or a life-partner, or a substitute mother for his son. Judy had assured him that she could accept that—but time had proved otherwise and her behaviour over Isabella had only confirmed his suspicions. But Judy was tenacious and Paulo too much of a gentleman to curtail the occasional maudlin phone-call.

'Did she want anything in particular?' he asked carefully.

Eddie pulled a face. 'Just the usual thing. She wanted to know where you were and I told her. But she went all quiet when I mentioned Bella.'

'Oh, did she?' questioned Paulo evenly.

'Mmm.' Eddie yawned. 'Papa—do I have to go to school tomorrow?'

Paulo frowned. 'Of course you do. It's term-time.'

'Yes, I know, but...' Eddie bit his lip. 'But I want to see Bella—and she went rushing off last time.'

'She won't be rushing anywhere,' said Paulo, but he could see from the expression in his son's eyes that Eddie remained unconvinced. And then he thought,

What the hell? What was one day out if it helped a ten-year-old accommodate this brand-new and unusual situation? 'Maybe,' he said as he picked up the wizard book which was wedged down the side of the bunk-bed. 'I said *maybe*!' His eyes crinkled. 'Want me to finish reading this?'

'Yes, please!'

'Where had we got to?'

'The bit where he turns his father into a toad by mistake!'

'Wishful thinking is that, Eddie?' asked Paulo drily as he found the place in the book and began to read.

But Eddie was fast asleep by the end of the second page, and Paulo turned off the light and tiptoed out of the room to find Isabella in a similar state, stretched out on the sofa, fast asleep, her hands clasped with Madonna-like serenity over her swollen belly.

It was the first time he had seen the tension leave her face, and he stood looking down at her for a long moment, realising how much she must have had to endure in that soulless house—pregnant and frightened and very, very alone. Her hair spilled with gleaming abandon over the velvet cushion which was improvising as a pillow and her thick dark lashes fanned her cheeks. She'd loosened the top couple of buttons of her dress, so that her skin above her breasts looked unbelievably fine and translucent—as if it were made of marble instead of flesh and blood. He could see the line of a vein as it formed a faint blue tracery above her heart, could see the rapid beating of the pulse beneath.

He heard a sound and looked up to find Jessie standing on the other side of the room, her face very thoughtful as she watched him studying the pregnant woman.

She looked as though she was dying to fire at least one question at him, but her remark was innocuous enough.

'The spare room is all ready,' she said, and waited.

'Thanks.' He turned away from where Isabella slept, and walked into the dining room to pour himself a whisky while he pondered on what he should do.

Jessie had been working for him ever since Elizabeth had died. Sometimes he'd thought that she must have been sent to him by angels instead of an employment agency. She'd been widowed herself, and knew that practical help was better than all the weeping and wailing in the world. She was young enough to be good fun for Eddie, but not so young that she felt she was missing out on life by looking after a child who was not her own.

He also knew that she was expecting some kind of explanation now, and knew that he owed her one.

And yet he did not want to gossip about Isabella while she lay sleeping. He took a sip of his whisky and raised dark, troubled eyes to where Jessie stood.

'I'll be off now,' she said. 'There's a salad in the fridge, if you're hungry.'

'We ate on the way home.' He nodded at the tray of crystal bottles. 'Stay for a drink?'

Jessie shook her head. 'No, thanks—I've got a date.'

'A *date*?'

Her smile was faintly reproving. 'Don't sound so shocked, Paulo—I know I'm on the wrong side of forty, but I'm still capable of having a relationship!'

It occurred to him that Jessie might fall in love. Might even leave him. And, oddly enough, the idea alarmed him far less than he would have imagined. 'Is it...serious?'

'Not yet,' she said quietly. 'But I think it's getting there.'

'Whoa! And there was me thinking you were in love with your work!'

'In your dreams!'

He drew a breath and followed her out to the front door, where he helped her into her coat and handed her her gloves. 'Listen, Jessie—'

She turned to look up at him. 'I'm listening.'

'About Isabella—'

She shook her head firmly. 'No, honestly. You don't have to tell me anything—and I won't ask you anything.' She screwed her face up uncomfortably. 'Well, maybe just one thing—but then you probably know what that is, already.'

His gaze was nothing more than curious. 'What?'

'Are you the father?'

He very nearly spat his whisky out, and it took him several seconds before he was ready to answer. 'Jessie—that's so outrageous, it's almost funny! Almost,' he added warningly and his dark eyes glittered with indignant question. 'You don't honestly think that, do you? That I would suddenly produce a child-to-be? That I would have been having a relationship with Judy, when all the time I had made another woman pregnant?'

'No, of course I don't.' Jessie shrugged and sighed. 'When you put it like that, I suppose the very idea is crazy. But isn't that what everyone else is going to think?'

'Why would they think that?' he growled. 'She's only twenty!'

'And you're only just thirty!' Jessie retorted. 'It's not exactly the age-gap from hell!'

'And I've known her since she was a child,' he said stubbornly.

'Well, she's certainly no child now!' retorted Jessie.

After she'd gone, he walked back into the sitting room to stand over the sleeping woman on the sofa once more, mesmerised by the soft movement of her breathing. No, Jessie was right. Isabella was certainly no child.

She'd relaxed into her sleep even more. Her arms were stretched above her head and a smile played around her lips—the first really decent smile he'd seen all day. Though maybe that wasn't so surprising, in the circumstances. Maybe sleep offered her the only true refuge at the moment. And he realised with a pang just how much he had missed that easy, soft smile.

Overwhelmed by a sense of deep compassion, he leaned over her and put his hand on her shoulder and gave it a gentle shake.

'Isabella?' he said quietly.

She didn't respond—not verbally, anyway. She murmured something incomprehensible underneath her breath, and wriggled deeper into the sofa, and the movement made the fabric of her maternity dress cling to her thighs.

Paulo swallowed.

Pushing against the sheen of the material, the bump of the baby could be seen in its true magnitude. She should have looked ungainly, but she looked nothing of the sort—she looked quite lovely, and he felt his body battling with his conscience as he gently shook her shoulder again, but she continued to writhe softly.

He felt desire shoot through him like an arrow—all the more piercing for its unexpectedness and its inappropriateness. And he must have made a small sound, because her eyelids fluttered half-open to stare at him.

And in the unreal world between waking and sleeping, it seemed perfectly natural for Paulo's darkly implacable face to be bent so close to her that for a moment it seemed as though he might kiss her. It was a lifetime's fantasy come true and she stretched her arms above her head in unconscious invitation.

'Paulo?' she whispered dreamily. 'What is it?'

He shook his head, telling himself that she had aroused in him feelings of protectiveness, nothing more. Nature was cunning like that—it made a woman who was ripe with child look oddly beautiful so that men would *want* to protect her. 'It's bedtime,' he responded sternly, but the trusting tremble of her lashes stabbed him in the heart, and made him ache in the most unexpected of places. 'You look like you need it. If you want, I can carry you.'

'Heavens, no—I'll walk,' she protested, wide awake now. 'I'm much too heavy to carry.'

'No, you're not—I bet you're as light as a little bird. Want to test me it out?'

'No,' she lied, and struggled up into a sitting position.

He helped her to her feet and put his hand in the small of her back to support her, just the way he had once done with Elizabeth.

Except that Elizabeth had been almost as tall as him— while Isabella seemed such a tiny little thing beside him. Why, she barely came up to his shoulder. And yet looks could be deceptive—he knew how tough she could be. You only had to see her astride an excitable horse, expertly subduing it into submission, to realise how strong she could be. He had never imagined that she could look almost frail.

'Come on,' he said softly. 'Lean against me.'

Too sleepy to refuse, she allowed him to guide her

upstairs and into a bedroom, where there was a large bed with a duvet lying invitingly folded back.

'Get undressed now,' he whispered, as she flopped down on the mattress and sighed.

'Nnnng!' She pillowed her head on her hands, and closed her eyes.

'Isabella!' he said sternly. 'Get yourself ready for bed, unless you want me to do it for you!'

Her eyes snapped open. This was no dream. Paulo was here. Right here. And he was threatening to undress her! 'I can manage. Really.'

He gave her a narrow-eyed look of assessment, only really believing her when she unclipped her gold wrist-watch and slid it down over the narrow wrist.

'Goodnight,' he said abruptly.

'Goodnight, Paulo.'

He left the door slightly ajar, so that the light from the corridor would penetrate the room if she woke. She would not flounder around frightened in the middle of the night in unfamiliar darkness.

But he was restless. Too restless for newspapers or the stack of paperwork he kept in the study, and which always needed attention. He drank some coffee and showered, and then slipped naked into bed, the cool sheets lying like silk against his bare skin while he lay and thought about the woman in the next room and who had made her pregnant. And how she could be persuaded to return to her own country—because surely that was the only rational option open to her.

He scowled up into the blackness, wondering why the idea of that should disturb him so.

In the end he gave up on sleep and decided that maybe he would tackle that paperwork after all. He pulled on a pair of jeans and shrugged a black T-shirt over his head, and on his way downstairs he paused briefly to look in on Isabella.

She was curled up on her side, facing the door, and from this angle the curve of her belly hardly showed at all. With the light from the corridor falling across the sculpted contours of her face and her lips slightly parted in sleep, it was easy to forget why she was here. Easy to imagine her being in a bed in his house for another reason entirely...

Paulo swiftly turned away and went downstairs.

He went through his papers on autopilot, gradually reducing the pile to a few sheets which his secretary could deal with tomorrow. He glanced down at his watch and yawned. *Today,* he should say. Better get to bed.

But he switched his computer on and began playing Solitaire.

He must have been dozing because he didn't hear the front door opening or clicking to a close. Nor did he hear soft footsteps approaching his study. In fact, the first indication that he had a visitor came from the sound of laboured breathing from just outside the door.

His eyes snapped open, his senses immediately on full alert, as he acknowledged that something had aroused him. He willed the aching fullness to subside.

'Bella?' he called softly. 'Is that you?'

'Sorry to disappoint you,' came an acid female reply. 'It's only me.'

He sat up straight as a tall, slim figure walked into the room and frowned at her in disbelief. *'Judy?'*

'Yes, Judy!' came the sarcastic reply. 'Why, did you think it was your little Brazilian firecracker?'

He reached out to click a further light on, his eyes briefly protesting against the bright glare as he stared at the woman standing uninvited before him.

The artificial light emphasised her pale-haired beauty—her long, willowy limbs and the pellucid blue eyes set in an alabaster skin. She wore jeans and an expensive-looking sheepskin jacket. And an expression he recognised instantly as a potent cocktail of lust and jealousy. He kept his face completely neutral.

'Hello, Judy,' he said softly, carefully. 'I wasn't expecting you.'

She raised her eyebrows and laughed. 'You made that obvious enough.'

He kept his voice steady. 'I didn't realise you still had a key.'

'That's what keeps life so interesting, isn't it, Paulo? These little surprises.'

He sighed. 'Judy, I don't want a scene.'

'No. It's pretty obvious from your greeting just what you *do* want!'

'Meaning?'

'Is that woman is staying here? She is, isn't she?'

'You mean Isabella?' he asked coldly.

Judy scowled, ignoring the warning note in his voice. 'You know damned well I do! You thought I was *her* when I came in, didn't you? ''Bella''! Well, I'm so sorry to disappoint you, Paulo! How long is she planning on staying for?'

Paulo didn't react. The only movement in his face was the dark warning which glittered from his eyes. 'I don't think that this is a good time to have this conversation,' he said carefully. 'Apart from which, it's really none of your business.'

For a moment her face looked almost ugly as different emotions worked their way across it.

'She's the reason you dumped me, isn't she?' she demanded. 'You were never the same after she came here to see you. I could see it in your eyes that day. You were really *hot* for her, weren't you, Paulo? In a way you never were for me. Not once.'

His mouth hardened as he realised that she had no idea that Isabella was pregnant. And he had no intention of telling her. He carried on as though she hadn't spoken. 'I'm actually very tired, so if you don't mind…'

Judy stiffened as she read the rejection in his features. 'What's she got that I haven't, Paulo?' she pleaded. 'Just tell me that.'

He shook his head. 'Go home,' he whispered. 'Go home now, before it's too late.'

Her eyes lit up as she completely misinterpreted his words. 'For what? Too late to resist me, you mean? Well, maybe I don't want you to resist me. Maybe I want what you're trying to resist, just as badly as you do. What does it matter? I won't tell.' She moved towards the desk and the overpowering scent of her perfume invaded his senses and deadened them. 'Come on, Paulo— what do you say? For old times' sake.'

He shook his head, felt distaste whipping up his spine like a ragged fingernail. 'No.'

'No?' She flicked her pale hair back. 'Sure?'

This really was astonishing, thought Paulo. A beautiful blonde begging him for sex. It was most red-blooded men's ideal fantasy and yet all he could think of was that she was going to wake the pregnant woman who lay sleeping upstairs.

'Quite sure. Keep your voice down.' He flattened his voice as the needs of his body fought with the demands of his mind. 'And I think it's better if you go right now.'

'And what if I stay and do…this…?' Her hand swooped towards him and he knew immediately just where she intended to touch him.

'I don't want you to.' With razor-sharp reflexes, he snapped his fingers around her wrist to stop her. *'I don't want you to,'* he repeated deliberately. 'Ever again. Got that?'

She stared into his eyes, like a woman who had never encountered rejection before and snatched her hand back. 'Why not?' she sneered. 'You want to do it with *Bella*, I suppose?'

He didn't have to tell her to get out; the look in his eyes must have done that effectively enough. He just heard her running down the hallway and slamming the front door so loudly that it echoed through the house like gunfire.

He waited until the automatic response of his body had died away completely, and he felt an ugly kind of taste in his mouth. Quietly, he turned the computer off and went to find himself a drink.

Barefooted, he went silently along to the kitchen where he poured himself a glass of water and stood drinking it, looking out of the window into the night sky. Outside, silver-white stars pin-pricked the darkened night and he found himself picturing Isabella's father's ranch in Vitória da Conquista. Where the stars were as big as lollipops—so bright and so close that you felt you could lean out and pluck them from the sky.

He pressed the empty water glass to his hot cheek as he anticipated the fireworks to come. What the hell was Isabella's father going to say when he discovered that his beloved daughter was going to have a baby? By a man she was refusing to name! He was going to be *absolutely furious*.

He was just thinking about going back to bed when he turned to see Isabella standing in the doorway, silently watching him.

She had changed into a big, white nightshirt and a pair of bedsocks and had plaited her hair, so that two thick, dark ropes hung down either side of her face. She looked impossibly sweet and innocent, making the swollen belly seem indecent in comparison.

'Did I wake you?' he asked. He saw the way she grimaced, then tried to turn it into a smile and he pulled a face himself. 'Obviously, I did.'

'I heard...er...noises. Then the door slammed.'

'And did it startle you?'

'Only for as long as it took me to realise where I was. But I probably would have woken at some point, in any case. Indigestion,' she said, in answer to the query in his eyes. 'It's the bane of late pregnancy.'

'I suppose it is,' he said slowly. He stared again at her bulging stomach. 'Would a glass of milk help?'

'Yes, please.'

'Sit down, then, and I'll fetch it for you.'

She pulled a chair out from under the kitchen table and negotiated herself into it, wriggling her toes around inside the roomy bedsocks.

Paulo reached into the fridge and poured her a big, creamy tumblerful, then leaned against the draining board and watched while she drank it. He found himself fascinated by the white moustache she left behind, and by the tiny pink tongue-tip which snaked out to lick it away. Who would ever have thought that a heavily pregnant woman could look so damned sexy? he wondered.

His wife had been sick for a lot of her pregnancy. The doctors had told him she was 'delicate'. Like a piece of Dresden china that he dared not touch for fear of breaking her. And yet Isabella looked real and very, very touchable.

Isabella could feel him watching her, and she tried to drink her milk unselfconsciously, but it was difficult. And she could feel the baby moving around at the same time as her breasts began to sting uncomfortably in a way she was certain had nothing to do with the pregnancy. What conflicting and confusing messages her body was sending out!

She put the half-empty glass down on the table with a clunk. 'Did...did Elizabeth have an easy pregnancy?'

Paulo frowned. 'No, not really. It didn't agree with her. She was very sick for the first five months or more.'

Her expectant look didn't waver. Here in the quietness of the night, it was easier to ask questions which had always seemed inappropriate before. 'You must miss her.'

He didn't answer for a moment. 'I did. Terribly, at first. But it was such a long time ago,' he said slowly. 'That sometimes it seems to have happened to another person. We were together for two years, and Lizzie's been dead for ten.'

'Doesn't Eduardo ever ask?'

'Sometimes.'

Isabella studied him. 'And does he have any contact with his mother's family?'

'A little,' he began, then suddenly his temper flared. 'What is this, Isabella?' he demanded, suddenly impatient. 'Truth or dare?' Women did not ask him about his wife—in fact, they did the very opposite. Ignored the few photographs which existed of Elizabeth with her infant son. Never asked the child any questions about his mother, as though they could not bear to acknowledge that he had loved a woman and had a child by her.

'You want to squeeze every painful fact out of me?'

he grated. 'Yet obstinately refuse to disclose the identity of your baby's father?'

'That's different.'

'Why?' he snapped.

'Because there's no point in your knowing,' she said stiffly. 'I told you. It's over.'

'So why this sudden interrogation? Is this one rule for you and another for me? Is that it?'

She shook her head. 'If I thought that telling you would do any good, then I would.'

'But you don't trust me not to use the information?' he probed softly.

'No, I don't,' she admitted.

For some inexplicable reason, he smiled. 'Then you are wise, *querida*,' he murmured. 'Very wise indeed.'

He saw the way that one plait moved like a silken rope over her breast when she lifted her head to meet his gaze head-on like that. 'Now go to bed, Bella,' he said roughly. 'You need your sleep.' And I need my sanity.

She paused by the door. He had warned her off prying, but there were some things she really *did* need to know. And if Paulo was in the habit of having late-night visits... 'Did I hear you talking to someone earlier?'

'I had an...unexpected visitor.' He gave a grim kind of smile. And anyway, what was the big secret supposed to be? 'It was Judy.'

'But I thought you said that it was over?' She'd blurted the indignant words out before she could consider their impact. Or the fact that she had no right to say them.

He knew it was a loaded question. Knew it and was surprised by it. No, maybe not completely surprised. 'It is.' He gave her a brief, hard look. 'She won't be coming back again.'

'Oh.' She kept her voice as expressionless as possible and hoped that her face did the same. 'Was it serious between the two of you? I suppose it must have been if she had a key.'

He gave a faint frown, tempted to dodge the question, knowing instinctively that the truth would hurt her. 'I don't do "serious" any more, Bella,' he told her quietly.

She felt her heart plummet. 'No. Right. Well, I guess it's time I went back to bed.'

Paulo's eyes narrowed with interest as he watched the interplay of emotions on her face. Maybe Judy had been more astute than he had given her credit for.

'I guess it is,' he agreed blandly. 'Goodnight, Isabella.'

CHAPTER FIVE

ISABELLA was woken by a timid knocking on her bedroom door, and she yawned as she picked up her wristwatch from the bedside locker.

Sweet heaven—it was nearly ten o'clock! She stretched beneath the bedclothes after the best night's sleep she had had since arriving in England. How wonderful to have the luxury of lying in. By now in the Stafford house she would have been up and running for three hours. She would have cooked breakfast and loaded the washing-machine and be just about to pick up the vacuum cleaner.

The knocking on the door grew louder.

She sat up in bed and smoothed her hands over her dishevelled plaits. 'Come in!' she called.

A small, dark head poked itself round the door. It was Eduardo. And she could see wariness and excitement on his face.

'Hello, Eduardo.' She smiled. 'Come on in!'

'Hello,' he said cautiously.

'Or should I call you Eddie? That's what Jessie calls you, isn't it? Would you prefer that?'

'Only in England.' He nodded. 'When we're in Brazil, you can call me my real name.' He stood there rather awkwardly. 'Shall I draw the curtains back?'

She sensed his diffidence and widened her smile. 'Would you mind? That would be wonderful—then I can see what kind of view I have!'

The pale, sharp light of winter came flooding into the

room as the curtains swished back to reveal the green blur of the distant park. Eddie turned round and Isabella patted the edge of the bed. 'Come and sit down over here. Or do you have to go to school?' She frowned down at her gold wristwatch. 'Aren't you a little late?'

'Papa said I can have the day off—to welcome you,' he added shyly.

'I'm honoured,' she replied softly and patted the mattress again. 'Come and sit down.'

He hesitated for one shy moment, then came over and did as she asked, glancing at the huge bump rather cautiously. 'Papa said you were going to have a baby.'

'That's right.' She supposed he must have told Eddie the evening before, when he'd gone in to read a bedtime story and she had been lying dozing on the sofa. She wondered what he'd said to the child. How he'd explained away the lack of a father. Maybe he'd turned it into a lecture on morality. 'I am.'

'Does it hurt?' he asked.

Isabella smiled. 'No. Why should it?'

'You must have to grow more skin?'

She laughed, and the movement made the baby start to protest. 'I've never thought about that, to be honest. The most painful thing is when it kicks. Sometimes it gets you right—' she clutched at her ribs and screwed up her face in an expression of mock-anguish '—here!'

'Maybe that means he'll be a football player,' suggested Eddie hopefully.

'But what if it's a girl?'

He shrugged. 'Then she can watch!'

'Or be the star of an all-girls team?'

'Nah!' Eddie shook his head decisively. 'Girls don't play football! Not properly, anyway!'

Isabella laughed, enjoying the comfort of the bed and

the room, and the winter sunshine which streamed into the room and made bright puddles of light on the crisp blue and white bedlinen. It was very obviously a spare room—well-decorated and luxuriously appointed, but with little in the way of personality stamped on it. A vase of flowers might help, she thought. Or would that just look as though she was taking up permanent residence?

'Papa sent me in to ask whether you like tea or coffee in the morning?'

She made a face. 'Your father asked *that*? Tell him that I drink only coffee in the mornings—and then it must only be Brazilian coffee!'

'Ah! Then I must be a mind-reader,' came a murmured boast and Paulo appeared, carrying a tray of the most wonderful-smelling coffee.

He glanced over to the bed, to where she sat with strands of dark-bronze hair escaping from her plaits; Eddie was perched on the bed next to her and Paulo's breath caught like grit in his throat.

They looked such a *unit* sitting there together, that for a moment he found himself imagining what life might have been like if Elizabeth had not died, an indulgence he rarely surrendered to. There might have been brothers and sisters for Eddie, and Eddie might have sat on the bed with his pregnant mother, just like that. He felt a great wave of sadness for the hole in his son's life. 'OK if I come in?'

'Of course it is.' But Isabella had noticed the swift look of pain and wondered what had put it there.

'Papa—Bella says the baby's kicking!'

'Well, that's what babies tend to do.'

'Did *I*?'

'Sure you did.' Paulo nodded, and put the tray down.

He had not foreseen that having a pregnant woman around the place would open up a new channel of thought for his inquisitive son. 'Your mother used to say that you were sure to be a star footballer when you finally made an appearance!'

'But that's what Isabella just said about *her* baby!'

Glittering black eyes connected with hers. 'Oh, did you?' he asked softly, as he lifted up the coffee pot and began to pour.

Isabella found herself wishing that she had leapt straight out of bed and replaited her hair. Or something. Not, she reminded herself, that she was in any kind of condition to go leaping anywhere. And not that Paulo would even notice if she had done. She took the coffee he offered her. 'Thanks.'

He searched her face for shadows, real and imagined, but he could see none. 'Sleep all right?'

'Mmm.' Eventually. She'd heard him moving restlessly in the next room for a while after they had gone their separate ways, and then the milk had made her sleepy.

Eddie looked up at his father. 'Where are we going today, Daddy?'

'Well, Isabella needs to see a doctor—'

'No, I don't—'

'Oh, yes, you do,' he argued.

'But I saw one last week!' she protested.

'Not in London, you didn't,' he pointed out. 'And you need to meet the doctor who will be delivering you. A Brazilian friend of mine.' He stirred sugar into his coffee. 'Who happens to be one of the country's finest obstetricians! I've already spoken to him.' He saw her mutinous expression and turned to his son with a smile. 'Go and fetch Isabella some crackers, would you, Eddie? Pregnant women need to eat when they wake up.'

Isabella put her cup down as the child jumped off the bed and ran from the room and fixed Paulo with a determined look. 'I am not so provincial that I need to have a fellow countryman deliver me, you know!'

'No. But why not make life a little easy for yourself?' His mocking expression seemed to indicate that it wasn't too late to start. 'You can speak to him in Portuguese and he will understand you.'

'But I'm bilingual!' she replied.

His stare was very direct; the mischief in his eyes unmistakable. 'Yes, I know you are. But I won't feel happy until I've had you checked over properly.'

'You make me sound like a car! Whichever doctor I decide to see is my business, Paulo—not yours.'

'Ah.' He glittered her a look. 'But you've made it my business.'

'No, you did that all by yourself! My father just asked you to look me up,' she argued. 'That was all. *You* were the one who insisted on bringing me back to your home.'

'And by agreeing to come, I'm afraid that you put yourself under my domain. Don't fight it, Bella,' he murmured softly, his eyes gleaming as he deliberately made his statement as ambiguous as possible. 'I feel responsible for your mental and physical welfare—and that automatically gives me certain rights.'

'Rights?' She stared at him, and an odd kind of excitement began to unfurl in the pit of her stomach. 'What sort of rights?'

He gave a slow smile because her reaction hadn't gone unnoticed. 'Such as making sure you look after yourself—which you haven't been doing up until now. Simple things like eating properly, and getting enough rest and fresh air.' He looked up as his son came back into the room, and his eyes were still glittering. 'Oh, and a little gentle exercise wouldn't hurt.'

Isabella wondered if she was going insane. She must be. His words seemed to be laden with sexual overtones this morning—and the look in his eyes only seemed to confirm it. She put her empty cup down, reminding herself that she knew nothing of men—and even less about a man like Paulo Dantas—the man they called *gato*.

He sipped his coffee and watched her over the rim of his cup. 'Now, *querida*,' he said softly. 'On the subject of baby equipment.'

Isabella looked at him blankly. 'Baby equipment? What about it?'

'Exactly! You don't have any, do you? No crib. No pram. No nappies, even. And even little babies need toys and stimulation.'

She shook her head. 'No, babies need roots and they need wings,' she contradicted dreamily. 'Anything else is just extra.'

'Very idealistic, Bella,' he said drily. 'And it makes for a good opt-out clause if you don't happen to like shopping. But where are they supposed to sleep?'

'Babies can sleep in drawers, if they need to!'

'*Can* they?' asked Eddie, who came back in, carrying a plate of dry crackers.

'Sure they can!' Isabella took a biscuit. 'When people lived in caves, they didn't have bassinets, did they?'

'When people lived in caves, the man's word was law—sounds like good sense to me,' said Paulo coolly. 'And as the man of the house I suggest we go out today and buy everything you need.'

'And can we go to the toyshop, Papa?' Eddie demanded eagerly.

'Provided Isabella isn't too tired.' He frowned as he handed her a cup of coffee. 'And, just out of interest, how were you planning to manage at the other place? Were you really planning to put the baby in a drawer?'

'Of course I wasn't.' She waited while the baby completed its three hundred and sixty-degree turn in her belly before replying. 'Mrs Stafford said I could use the twins' old baby stuff.' Tired-looking pieces of equipment which had been stacked in a disused garage and covered with dust and cobwebs. 'She said they would clean up perfectly!'

'I'll bet she did,' said Paulo grimly. 'Well, why don't you get showered and dressed.' He glanced down at his watch. 'Your doctor's appointment is at midday.'

He was certainly showing a very bossy side to his nature, thought Isabella as she stood beneath the power-shower in her luxurious en-suite, which gushed as efficiently as a small waterfall. She savoured every moment of it, washing her hair without difficulty.

She lumbered back into the bedroom afterwards and slipped her other maternity dress on. She'd only bought a couple—unwilling and unable to invest money in clothes she would never wear again. But at least Paulo hadn't seen her in this one before, and its cheerful yellow colour warmed the pale olive of her skin and brought out the red highlights in her dark hair.

Everything took such a long time when you were this pregnant. She sat down heavily at the dressing-table and picked up her hairbrush, wondering if she had the energy to dry her wet hair, strand by laborious strand.

A movement at the open door attracted her attention and she glanced up to see Paulo reflected back at her— and it was with a sense of guilt that she noticed how the dark trousers moulded themselves so beautifully to the jut of his hips and the powerful line of his thighs. Surely she shouldn't be thinking about his *legs* at a time like this?

'Want me to do that for you?' he asked.

'Dry my hair?'

The eyes gleamed with the faintest hint of laughter. He had seen just where her gaze had focussed itself. 'That's what I meant.' He walked over to the mirror and plucked the silver-backed hairbrush from her hand. 'Relax,' he soothed, as he stroked the bristles down through the resisting locks. 'Come on. Relax.'

Relax? How could she possibly do that when his pelvis was on a level with her back, and the reflection of his black eyes was mocking her in the mirror?

But the soothing movement of the brush lulled her into a glorious state of peace and calm. Ironic, really, considering just how precarious her position was. She guessed that this was what they called false security, and let her gaze drift upwards to clash with the hard glitter of ebony once more.

'You know, I'm going to have to ring your father today, Bella. He'll be expecting me to get back to him and wondering why I haven't. And you'll need to speak to him yourself.'

She kept the tremor of nerves away. 'Not today.'

'When, then?'

'Tomorrow. When I feel…calmer.'

'You think twenty-four hours will make such a difference?' he demanded.

'I don't know. I just haven't made up my mind what to tell him.'

'How about the truth?' he suggested sardonically. 'Or is that something which is beyond you?'

'I haven't told him any lies!' she defended.

He gave a short laugh. 'You just ran away instead. Well, I'm afraid that it won't do, Bella!'

She stiffened. 'What do you mean, it won't do? It'll do if I say it will!'

'Not if I decide to tell him myself,' he said silkily.

'You wouldn't do that!'

'Oh, wouldn't I?' he questioned softly, but a note of steel had entered his voice. 'Believe me, I would do whatever I felt necessary to guarantee the well-being of you *and* your baby.'

'Even if it was contrary to what I wanted?'

'Your wants are of no particular concern to me!' he snapped. 'Your *needs* are far more relevant! Have you stopped to think about the things that could go wrong?'

Her golden eyes widened in alarm. 'Such as what?'

He drew in a deep breath. He didn't want to put the fear of God into her—but that did not mean she could bury her head in the sand, either. 'You're young and fit and healthy—but pregnancy carries its own risks. You're an intelligent woman, Bella—you know that. Your father needs to know about the baby.'

He did not want to spell it out, that if some calamity befell her during labour... He gripped the hairbrush so hard that his knuckles whitened. 'That doesn't mean you have to tell him who the father is,' he added gently. Not yet, anyway.

He hoped that she wasn't about to get a rude awakening and that her airy assurance that she would feel herself after the birth proved to be the case. He wondered how she would cope if she fell foul of the baby blues. Or how he would cope...

He picked up the hairdryer and blasted the thick, dark mass with warm air until her hair hung in a shimmering sheet all the way down to her waist. 'Let's see what the doctor says first,' he said evenly.

She met his eyes in alarm, realising that whatever she said he would blithely ignore it, if he thought that it was in her best interests to do so.

She thought about arguing with him, but instinct told her that it would be a waste of time. And besides, deep down she knew he was right. 'OK,' she sighed.

He carefully caught up the great weight of hair and tied it at the base of her neck with a saffron-coloured ribbon which matched her dress. 'I think I like it when you're acquiescent,' he murmured.

She met his eyes in the mirror. 'Don't hold your breath!'

The doctor's suite of rooms was in an upmarket patch of Knightsbridge, and Isabella wondered how much this was all costing. But when she tentatively broached the subject of cost with Paulo, she was silenced by an arrogant wave of his hand.

The doctor insisted on conducting the entire examination in Portuguese, despite all Isabella's protestations that her English was fluent.

'But it is the mother-tongue.' The doctor smiled sentimentally. 'And particularly appropriate for the mother-to-be. Do you want Paulo to stay with you?' he added.

Isabella shot Paulo a look of pure horror.

'No, I won't be staying,' answered Paulo smoothly, answering her furious query with an unconcerned smile. 'Isabella is by nature a traditionalist, aren't you, *querida*? She knows how easily men faint!'

She didn't trust herself to reply, just gave him a frozen smile before the nurse popped the thermometer into her mouth.

The doctor was ruthlessly thorough, making little

clicking noises as he listened to the baby's heartbeat with an old-fashioned trumpet, as well as the most high-tech equipment she had ever seen.

She dressed again and sat down in front of the doctor and Isabella didn't realise how nervous she was until he looked at her over the top of his spectacles and gave her a look which managed to be both reassuring and alarming.

'Everything is fine—but there is room for improvement! You have not been resting enough!' he announced sternly. 'And you are a little underweight. You must look after yourself, do you understand?'

'Yes, Doctor,' she answered meekly.

Paulo was ushered back into the room and the doctor spread out some shiny black and white ultrasound photos on the desk.

'See what a beautiful baby you have.' He smiled at them both.

Isabella swallowed as she looked down at the tiny limbs. So perfect. A lump rose in her throat and when she looked up it was to see Paulo's eyes on her—the dark gaze oddly soft and luminous.

'A very beautiful baby,' agreed Paulo softly, giving her such a blindingly brilliant smile that she felt quite dizzy—so dizzy in fact, that she couldn't make out a word the doctor was saying to him.

In fact, the nurse was busy chattering herself. She wanted to know everything. Which part of Brazil did Isabella come from?

'From Bahia.'

'Very beautiful,' the nurse replied. 'The Land of Happiness.' It seemed that she had taken holidays there as a child. She glanced down at one of the ultrasound photos Isabella was clutching, and smiled. How long had she known Paulo for?

'Oh, most of my life,' Isabella replied automatically.

'*That* long?' The nurse gave a dreamy sort of sigh.

'Mmm. Obviously, I was a child for a lot of that time.'

'Ah, of course! He is a handsome man—a *very* handsome man,' whispered the nurse, though Isabella wasn't sure whether this was at all professional. '*Gato,*' she finished huskily, with an admiring look at Paulo's hips.

'What was the nurse saying to you?' Paulo asked her, as they walked out of the clinic towards the car.

'Oh, nothing much,' replied Isabella vaguely. She certainly wasn't going to boost his ego by telling him that the nurse had unerringly hit on his Brazilian nickname. 'What was the doctor saying to *you*?' she asked him suspiciously.

He hesitated, and waited until she was safely strapped into the low, deep blue car before he told her.

'He said that between the two of us, we had created a fine Latino baby!'

She felt a pang of something approaching wistfulness. 'Oh, Paulo, he *didn't*!'

'Yes, *querida*—he did. I suppose it was a natural enough assumption to make under the circumstances.'

'So why didn't you explain that you weren't the father?'

'And what would you have me tell him instead?' he questioned, his voice chilly now. 'That you're refusing to say who the father is?'

'That *is* my prerogative.'

'Though maybe you don't even know yourself?' he challenged insultingly.

Isabella felt the blood rush to her face. Is that what

he thought of her? That any number of men could qualify for paternity? 'Of course I know who the father is!'

A look of triumph flared darkly in his eyes and she realised too late that she had walked into some kind of trap.

Paulo's voice was deceptively soft. 'But he doesn't know about the baby either, does he? You haven't told him, have you, Isabella?'

Her lips trembled, but she could not afford to break down. Not now, when she had nursed her secret so carefully and for so long. 'No, I haven't.' She found herself imprisoned in the searchlight of his keen, dark gaze.

'Why not?'

She had kept the identity of her baby's father secret from everyone. Because the moment she gave a name to either Paulo—or Papa—she could just imagine the outcome. Somehow they would track Roberto down, demand that he take an active role in her child's life. Isabella shuddered. Never! 'I don't have to answer that,' she said.

'No, of course you don't. But don't you think that he—as the father—has a right to know? And not just a right—a *responsibility* to share in the child's upbringing.'

'No! Because it's over! There's no *point* in telling him!'

But even as she spoke she felt guilt descend on her like a dark cloud. She wasn't being fair to Paulo—allowing him to pay for everything and allowing him to care for her, too. He had rescued her. Given her sanctuary. A sanctuary she hadn't realised she had needed, until it had been forced upon her. And maybe that gave *him* some rights.

Paulo turned the key in the ignition with an angry jerk,

wondering why he almost preferred to think that she *didn't* know who the father was. As if it was somehow more acceptable to imagine her having some regrettable one-night stand with far-reaching consequences, than the alternative. Had she loved the man responsible? Did she love him still?

Perhaps her statement that it was over was just a ruse. She could be using the baby as a way to lever herself back into the man's life. Planning to just turn up and present a child who crooned so sweetly in her arms. Some proud, dark lover, maybe, who would be swayed by the sudden production of his own flesh and blood. It wouldn't be the first time it had happened.

Isabella sneaked a look at the forbidding set of his jaw, and her heart sank even more. To Paulo, it must seem as though she was letting her child's father get off scot-free. Yet it was not quite as simple as that. The situation was bad enough—but if she tried imagining a future which involved Roberto—it made her feel quite ill. A man she didn't love and who didn't love *her*. What effect could he have on her life, other than disaster?

'Paulo?' she asked tentatively, but he smacked the flat of his hand down on the steering wheel in frustration.

'I never had you down for such a coward!' he stormed. 'What do you think is going to happen after the birth?'

'I don't know!' she answered back, and right then she didn't care—even that he had called her a coward—because a band of steel had tightened and stretched across her abdomen, and she felt her face distort with discomfort.

One look at her white face and Paulo's rage instantly evaporated. 'It's not the baby, is it?' he demanded.

She panted shallowly, the way she had been taught. 'No, I don't think so.'

He changed down a gear. 'Sure?'

She nodded. 'It's just one of these—' She struggled to remember the English for the unfamiliar medical term. 'Braxton-Hicks contractions—nature's rehearsal for the real thing.' She pressed her hot face onto the cool of the car window and gulped, hoping that Paulo wouldn't notice she was precariously close to tears.

But he did. He noticed most things. And as a way of bringing his interrogation to a close, her threatened tears proved extremely effective. He felt an impotent kind of rage and anger slowly unfurling in the pit of his stomach, and he was longing to take it out on someone. Or something.

If she hadn't been pregnant he might just have pulled into a layby and treated her to the kind of kiss he felt she deserved, and they both needed. He felt the first warm lick of desire and wondered grimly what masochistic tendency had pushed him towards *that* line of thinking.

If he had been on his own, he might have taken the car to the nearest motorway and driven it as fast as was safe. As it was, he didn't dare—one bump and her face might take on that white, strained look again. He slowed right down and negotiated the roads back to the house with exaggerated care.

Isabella had recovered her equilibrium by the time they got back to the house, but Paulo was busy treating her like an invalid. He made her eat an omelette and salad, then insisted that she lie down for a rest.

'But I'm not tired!'

'Really?' He cocked a disbelieving eyebrow at her.

'I'm fine,' she insisted, even while she allowed him

to crouch down by her feet to slip her shoes off. 'Honestly.'

'Well, you don't look fine.' He propelled her gently back against the stack of pillows. 'You look worn out.'

Isabella wriggled her head back against the pillow, and stared up into the glittering black eyes. 'Anyway, you promised Eduardo we could buy toys today—he was looking forward to it.'

'And we can. But only if you sleep first,' he ordered firmly. He brushed a damp lock of the bronze-black hair away from her cheek and carefully extracted the photos of the baby from where they lay clutched tightly between her fingers.

'That's bribery,' she objected muzzily.

'So what if it is?' came the soft rejoinder. 'Remember what the doctor told you.'

He glanced in on her more than once, telling himself that he was just making certain that the pains *had* been a false alarm.

But if he was being truthful he *enjoyed* watching her as she lay sleeping. And, if he examined his conscience, wasn't it erotic? The steady rise and fall of her breasts, so full and ripe and hard. The way the dark fringes of her eyelashes brushed over the flushed curve of her cheeks. The firm swell of the child as it grew within her. Look but don't touch. Of course it was erotic.

When Isabella awoke she felt much better. She slapped cold water on her face and brushed her teeth and went to find Paulo and his son sitting at the dining-room table, playing Scrabble.

Paulo looked up and gave her a long, searching stare, then nodded his head as if satisfied. 'That's better,' he murmured.

'Bella!' exclaimed Eddie, his face lighting up. 'Papa

said I wasn't to wake you! He said that you needed your sleep.'

'And he was right.' Her cheeks were flushed as she bit back a yawn. 'I did.'

'See how tolerant I can be, Bella,' Paulo said softly. 'When some people might find the urge to say, "I told you so"!'

'Very tolerant,' she agreed gravely, relieved that his black mood of earlier seemed to have subsided.

'And he says we can go and choose toys for the baby if you're well enough. Are you, Bella?'

Paulo was on his feet. 'Shush, Eddie,' he murmured. 'Bella has already had a trip to the doctor's this morning. We might have to put the toys on hold until another day.' Night-dark eyes captured her gaze. 'How do you feel?'

'Absolutely fine. I'm looking forward to it.'

'Very well. We will have a leisurely afternoon in the toy-shop.' He rose to his feet like some sleek, black panther. 'On the condition that you take it easy if I tell you to.'

She opened her mouth to point out that he wasn't her personal physician, but the warning gleam in his eyes made her change her mind. 'Very well,' she agreed demurely. 'I'll go and get ready.'

He chose one of the capital's biggest children's stores, where he seemed hell-bent on buying the place up and it was Isabella who had to restrain him.

Having rather distractedly looked round the place at baby paraphernalia which still seemed so *alien* to her, she placed her hand restrainingly on his arm. 'I just need a small pram that can double as a carry-cot, Paulo— nothing more for the time being.'

He stared down at the slim, ringless fingers as they

rested on the dark blue wool of his overcoat. 'What about a crib? And a high-chair?'

She shook her head before he could recite the entire contents of the shop to her. 'No, none of those. Not yet. They take up too much room and the baby can sleep in the pram until...' Her voice tailed off.

His eyes narrowed. 'Until you fly home to Brazil?'

She tried to imagine it, and couldn't. Tried to imagine staying here with Paulo—and that was even harder. 'I guess so. Oh, look—the assistant is coming over.'

His mouth flattened with irritation as the sales assistant fluttered to dance attention on his every word.

Isabella let him buy a baby-seat for the car, a drift of cashmere blankets and a tape of 'mood-music' to play to the baby.

She was caught between delight and protest. 'It isn't necessary,' she began, but the look of determination on his face made her give up.

At last they went to find Eduardo, who was totally engrossed in a train set in the toy department. He looked up as they approached, and his face fell. '*Oh!* Can't I stay here for a bit longer, Papa?'

'Sure you can,' grinned his father. 'Come on, Isabella—let's wander round and see what the fashionable baby is playing with these days!'

She'd planned to say yes to only the simplest and most inexpensive of the toys, deliberately telling herself that manufacturers were making a fortune out of bits of plastic. But, even so, they were surprisingly seductive and her attention was caught by a pyramid of stuffed animals in pale shades of pastel.

'And all colour co-ordinated—especially for the nursery,' said Paulo. He held up two teddy-bears, one pink and one blue, and waggled them like semaphores, managing to attract looks of interest from most of the women in the shop. 'So what are you hoping for, Bella—a boy or a girl?'

It was an innocent question which every mother-to-be in the world was asked. But no one had ever asked Bella before. Maybe they had been too embarrassed. Perhaps people thought that an unplanned pregnancy for a single girl meant that you didn't have the normal hopes and fears for your baby. But Paulo's words sparked some complex and primitive chain of emotions which included hope and despair and a terrible feeling of regret. As if they were a normal, expectant couple and Paulo really *was* her baby's father.

Oh, if only, she thought longingly as her field of vision dissolved into a helpless blur of longing. If only.

'Isabella?' His voice seemed to come from a long way off. She tried to say something, but her stilted words came out as nothing more than a jerky wobble. 'Isabella? What is this?'

'N-nothing.'

He saw the bright glare of tears which had turned her eyes into liquid gold. Her mouth began to tremble and he acted purely on instinct. They were standing beside a large red play-tent, and he simply flicked the flaps back and pulled her inside, where it was mercifully empty. Into their own private world, and into his arms where she burrowed through the warmth of his coat, letting her tears fall like raindrops onto his silk shirt.

He could feel her warm breath shuddering against his chest as she drooped her hands softly over his shoulders, and he felt an overpowering urge to tightly cradle her.

It was a surreal setting. They were bathed in a soft red light which made the inside of the tent almost womblike. 'W-we can't stay here,' she husked, a hint of quiet hysteria breaking through the blur of her tears.

'We can stay anywhere we damned well please!' he contradicted on a silken whisper. 'But quietly. Quietly, Bella. Do not excite yourself...or the baby.' Or me, he thought, with a sudden guilty realisation.

Her huge belly was pushing against him, so close that he could feel the baby as it moved inside her. But instead of acting as a natural deterent he found the action one of unbearable intimacy. It was comfort he intended to give her. Not this...this...powering of his heart so that it pounded hotly inside his head and his groin.

He deliberately made the gesture more avuncular, smoothing the flat of his hand down over her hair, fluidly stroking her head as if she were a Siamese cat, while the tears continued to soak through his shirt and onto his shoulder.

And it wasn't until the flow had abated and he had traced one last glimmering teardrop away with the tip of his finger, that he used that same finger to lift her chin, imprisoning her in the sweet, dark fire from his eyes.

'Want to talk about it?' he murmured.

What—and tell him that she wished he *was* the man who had caused life to spring within her? Little could terrify a man who didn't 'do' serious, more than that. She shook her head. 'I'm overwrought,' she said. 'It's a very—' and she gulped '—emotional time.'

'You're telling me,' he said grimly.

'Oh, Paulo!'

'I know.' He tightened his grip. She felt so warm and trembling and vulnerable in his arms. So small. Tiny, almost. What else could he do but carry on holding her like this? This was a hug she needed, he realised. That he seemed to need it too was what troubled him. 'What is it?' he asked her in her own language, feeling her breath warm his chest as she attempted to speak.

'I'm s-so s-sorry!'

He frowned, as he wiped a tear-soaked lock of hair away from her forehead. 'You've got nothing to be sorry for.'

'I got pr-pregnant, didn't I?'

His stare was laser-sharp. His need to know momentarily overrode his desire to be gentle with her. 'Deliberately?' he questioned. '*Was* it a gamble you took, Bella? As a way of keeping a man who perhaps didn't love you as much as you loved him?'

She gazed at him, shocked. 'No, of course not!' But by a man I didn't love. And she couldn't tell him that, could she? Because if she admitted that, then it would make the consequences of her act even harder to bear. At least love would have justified the whole wretched mess.

His eyes narrowed with alarming perception. 'Even if you *do* regret the act, Bella, you must learn to accept the consequences. Otherwise you will suffer, and so will the baby. Here.' And he smoothed away the last strand of hair, which had escaped from its confining bow. 'Come on, now—we're going home.'

He demanded that Eduardo make sure she stayed sitting on one of the carved wooden benches which adorned the shop's lavish entrance hall, while he brought the car round to the front of the building.

In her weakened state, she watched him. Watched his muscular grace and confident stride. He seemed quite oblivious to the fact that he could stop the traffic. Literally.

He arrogantly stepped in front of the traffic and no one dared not to obey him as he raised an imperious hand in command. But several cars had slowed down so much that they were almost stationary anyway—eager, no doubt to watch the spectacular-looking man with the brooding features as he helped the pale and pregnant woman into the car.

CHAPTER SIX

'BED!' Paulo insisted, just as soon as they arrived home.

'But—'

'Bed!' he repeated grimly. 'From now on we obey the doctor to the letter. He said you needed rest—and that's what I intend to make sure you get.'

One look at his expression told her that to put up a fight would be a waste of her time and energy, so she crept away to her room, where the bed was almost as welcoming as his embrace in the shop had been. The pillow felt soft against her cheek, and as sleep enfolded her, she remembered the way he had held her, with concern softening the brilliance of the dark eyes.

He brought her soup and toast and fruit for supper, and afterwards she slept on. As if her body was greedily sucking up every bit of relaxation it had been denied during her stay at the Staffords'.

She slept right through the night still tantalised by the memory of that hard, beautiful face and awoke to the sound of silence, which made her think that perhaps the flat was empty. But when she had showered and dressed, she found Paulo lying stretched out on the sofa in the sitting room.

He looked more relaxed than she had ever seen him, his dark hair all rumpled as it rested against a silken cushion. A newspaper was spread out over his bent knees and the jeans clung like syrup to his muscular thighs. Her heart crashed painfully against her ribs and the baby kicked against her, as if objecting. She took a deep, calming breath.

'Hello, Paulo.'

He glanced up from the newspaper, thinking how warm and soft she looked, all breathless and sparkly eyed. And how that innocent-looking white blouse provided the perfect backdrop for the thick, dark curls. He found himself wishing that he could reach out and untie the ribbon which confined them and let the whole damned lot tumble down and spill like satin around her shoulders.

'Well, good morning,' he said thickly, and put the paper down. 'Or should I say good afternoon?'

Her breath seemed to have caught somewhere in her throat. 'I overslept again.'

'That's good.'

'Have you eaten breakfast?'

'Not yet. I was waiting for you. Then I started reading and forgot about it.' He stretched his arms and stood up. 'I'll make it.'

'Where's Jessie?'

'She's gone shopping,' he replied, without missing a beat. He had sent the housekeeper out over an hour ago. There were a few things he was planning to say to Isabella today, and he wanted to do so in private. And if Jessie were there she would inhibit him. Because for the first time since Elizabeth's death, he had felt a tiny bit *crowded* by the woman who had worked for him for so long and so tirelessly. And he couldn't quite decide whether it was all tied up with Isabella's presence, or by the fact that Jessie now had a man.

Jessie's attitude had changed. And it wasn't so much the things she said—more the things she *didn't* say. The pursed lips. The raised eyebrows. The knowing smiles.

As if she knew some mysterious secret that she was keeping from him. And he was damned if he was going to ask her what the hell it was.

Isabella glanced at the newspaper headlines, but the drama of world news held little interest for her. She supposed it was the same for all women at this stage in their pregnancy—her world had telescoped right down into this baby inside her.

It was almost lunchtime by the time they sat down to eat, and Paulo waited until she had munched her way through a pastry before delivering the first part of the little lecture he intended to give, no matter how much she fluttered those big amber eyes at him.

'I want to talk to you about yesterday, Bella.'

Her coffee suddenly lost all its appeal. 'What about it?'

'You were in a virtual state of collapse in the shop,' he accused, looking at her as fiercely as if she had set out deliberately to do it!

'It won't happen again, I promise.'

'Damned right it won't! Because there will be no more all-day excursions, that's for sure! Dr Cardoso has agreed he will see you here at the house in future.' He pushed a dish of fruit across the table towards her and, to avoid a lecture on supplementing her diet with vitamins, she obediently took an orange.

'I should not have trailed you halfway around London the way I did,' he snapped.

Isabella slowly began to peel her orange, tempted to point out that he hadn't had to drag her screaming, but one look at his face told her not to bother. 'Finished?'

'No. Not yet.' He watched her pop a juicy segment in between her lips and swallowed down a sensation which came uncomfortably close to lust. 'In future, you will rest when I think you need to rest, and you will eat properly.'

She met his eyes with amusement. 'Oh, will I?'

'Yes, you will,' came the silky promise. 'You'd better make the most of this enforced leisure, Bella—God only knows it will be over soon enough!' His eyes were deadly serious now. 'Are you *listening* to me, Bella? Do you understand what I'm saying?'

'Of course I do.' She lifted up the jug. 'Coffee?'

'Please.' He hadn't finished yet, but he let her attempt to distract him.

She poured him a cup, thinking that this was what living with a man must be like. The small intimacies. The shared breakfasts. Her eyes strayed to the triangle of flesh at his neck which was exposed by an open button and she found herself wondering what it would be like to slowly unbutton that shirt, to lay bare the skin beneath and touch its silken surface with the tips of her fingers... And she wondered, too, whether it was madness or just depravity to yearn for someone while she carried another man's child. 'More toast?' she asked, her cheeks going pink with guilt.

'No, thanks,' he said, knowing that she was studying him, and *liking* it—even though he was uncomfortably aware of the irony of their situation. He wasn't in the habit of having breakfast with women. He had always insisted on eating the first meal of the day alone, or with his son, no matter who he had spent the night before with—or how wonderful it had been. It had been a strict rule, necessary to his son's well-being and security. His girlfriends hadn't liked it—but none of them had been willing to risk making a fight of it.

He found himself studying *her*, his gaze mesmerised by the full, tight swell of her breasts.

Sitting there, with her white cotton blouse straining across the bump of baby and without a scrap of make-up on her face, she looked the antithesis of the glamorous women who had passed through his life after the death of his wife. The cool, pale-blonde beauties with their enigmatic smiles.

And if anyone had suggested that he might find himself physically attracted to a woman who was pregnant with another man's child, he might have seriously questioned their sanity.

So how was it that he found he wanted to run the tip of his tongue all the way along that deep cleft which formed such an erotic shadow between her ripe, swollen breasts? He tried to quash the slow, sweet burn of desire as he met her expectant golden eyes but his mouth felt sandpaper-dry.

He glittered her a look of warning across the table. 'Today you *must* speak to your father—you can't put it off any longer. And the truth, Bella—because nothing else will do. He needs to know that you're going to have a baby and that in a couple of weeks time he will become a grandfather.'

A segment of orange slipped unnoticed from her hand. 'Paulo, I told you—I *can't*!' She couldn't bear the inevitable hurt—the disappointment which would surely follow. She loved her father and the bond between them was close. Or had been.

'You can't put it off any longer, I know that,' he said grimly. A combination of frustration and a sudden irrational fear that something might happen to her during the birth made Paulo's temper begin an inexorable simmer towards boiling point. 'Why can't you? What's stopping you? Are you frightened of his anger? Is he such a tyrant that you daren't tell him? What is the worst thing that could happen, Bella?'

'Let me spell out the stark facts for you,' she whispered. 'I am an only child. The only daughter. All my father's hopes and dreams rest with me—'

'I know all this.'

'Then surely you can understand that I can't just let him down?'

He hardened his heart against the misty blur of her eyes. 'It's a little late in the day for that, surely?'

'Your will is very formidable, Paulo,' she told him quietly. 'But even you can't impose it on me.'

He pushed his chair back and stood up. 'No, you're right—I can't,' he said coldly. 'But if you won't tell him today, then I *will*. I've told you what I think. End of subject.' He began to move towards the door.

She looked up in alarm. 'Where are you going?'

'Anywhere, just so long as it's out of here and away from the crazy thinking that masquerades as logic inside that head of yours!' he snapped. He saw her soft mouth pucker, irritated by the way the little movement stabbed at his conscience. 'Call me if you need me—I'll be working in my study. You know where the phone is!' With that he left the room, closing the door behind him with an exaggerated softness.

Left on her own, Isabella was restless. She cleared away their breakfast things and then wandered around aimlessly, putting off the inevitable moment. It was a huge, sprawling house and yet the walls closed in on her like a prison. She forced herself to curl up on the sofa and channel-hopped the TV stations for a while, but nothing grabbed her attention enough to draw her in. There just seemed to be inane game-shows and cookery programmes which didn't seem to teach you anything about cookery.

She found herself looking out of the window at the rain which lashed relentlessly against the pane and a deep, aching part of her knew that Paulo was right. That a baby was not a secret you could keep hidden for ever.

She *should* ring her father. Take all her courage and tell him.

Pity there were no books you could study to prepare for moments such as these. What should her opening line be? 'Papa, you know you always used to talk about becoming a grandfather—'

She shook her head and went back over to the sofa, glancing at her wristwatch. It would be lunchtime now at home, and her father would be tucking into a large plate of beans and rice and meat with vegetables. She dampened down a sudden pang of homesickness. Not a good time to ring. She would try later—after the siesta.

She must have drifted off to sleep herself, because she was woken up by the sound of a distant ringing, and then the click of a door opening, and when she opened her eyes it was to see Paulo standing looking down at her, his face tight and white and strained with an unbearable kind of tension.

She opened her eyes immediately. 'Paulo? What is it? What's happened?'

'I think you'd better come and speak to your father.'

She blinked at him, still befuddled. 'Did he phone?'

'Bella! This has gone on for long enough. You've got to start some kind of dialogue with him—and you can start *right now*!'

She levered herself up with difficulty.

'I'm waiting until after his siesta,' she yawned. 'I'll ring him then.'

He shook his head and his voice sounded odd. Quiet and controlled, but odd. 'I don't think you understand. You're too late. We've moved beyond the stage of being hypothetical. Your father is on the telephone, waiting to speak to you.'

'He can't be!'

'I can assure you that he is.'

The urgent pitch of his voice told her something else, too. 'He knows about the baby?' she asked him tonelessly.

'What do you think?'

She rose to her feet, putting her hand out onto the arm of the sofa to steady herself. 'You told him, didn't you?'

His gaze was steady. 'I had to.'

'Oh, no, you didn't!' she breathed in disbelief. 'You were just playing God, weren't you? You decided! You just went straight ahead and did exactly what you thought best—'

'Isabella.' He interrupted her with an icy clarity which stopped her in her tracks. 'Your father was worried sick—wondering why you hadn't got back to him. He asked me explicitly whether anything was wrong. So what did you want me to do? Compound what is going to happen anyway with a lie? How would that make me look?'

'That's all you care about, is it? How *you* look?'

He shook his head. 'Believe it or not, I care about you—I always have done. Why else would I have brought you back here?' he put in drily. 'But try putting yourself in my shoes and you'll realise you're not being fair. I owe it to your father, after all he has done for me, to tell him the *truth*! How could I look him in the eye if I had done otherwise? I am thinking only of your welfare, Bella, truly.'

He paused for a moment to let the impact sink in, aware that he was hurting her—maybe even frightening her—but even more aware that it was time she faced up to facts. 'You are acting like a child. It is time to face the music, *querida*.' He gentled his voice. 'Now, your father is waiting, impatient for the answers to his questions. I suggest you go along to my study and provide them for him. Go on.'

She knew then that she could not put this off any longer. She was beaten. And ashamed. She had let them both down—more than that—her stubborness and her cowardice had made a difficult situation even worse.

She stared up into Paulo's eyes, searching for something…anything. Some sign that she was not all alone, and the faint black gleam of empathy there was the only thing which gave her courage to do as he said.

Walking tall and very straight, she went into his study, where the telephone receiver was lying amidst the heap of paperwork which littered his desk. She picked it up with a hand which was oddly steady.

'Papa?' she breathed.

It was her father as she had never heard him before, his voice distorted with a kind of dazed disbelief.

'Bella, please tell me this isn't true,' he began.

'Papa,' she swallowed, but that was all she could get out.

'So it's true!' There was a short, terse exclamation, as if her inability to speak had damned her. 'You're *pregnant*,' he accused in a low voice.

There was no place left to go. No hiding place. The steel door of the prison clanged shut behind her. 'Yes,' she whispered. 'Yes, Papa—I'm afraid I am.'

In the seconds it took to confirm his fears, his voice seemed to have aged by about ten years. *'Meu Deus,'* he said heavily. 'I should have realised that something was the matter! Your explanation why you wanted to leave college never really convinced me, not in my heart. You were doing so well. *I should have realised!*'

'Papa, I didn't think—'

'No!' He cut across her words with uncharacteristic impatience. 'It is *me* who didn't think—*me* who has let your poor, dear mother down and failed as a parent.'

This was worse than unbearable. 'That's not true and you know it! You've been the best father there ever could have been.' She sucked in a painful breath. 'Papa, I'm so sorry.'

There was a short, strained silence and she could almost hear her father struggling to gain control over his composure.

'*You're* sorry?' The voice changed. 'But you are not the only one who is to be held accountable, are you, Bella? What of the...father—' he bit the word out with difficulty '—of your baby?'

'What about him?' A shadow fell over the desk, and she looked up into a silent black stare and the hand which was holding the receiver began to shake. 'I don't want to talk about him.'

Her father ignored her. 'Well, I do.'

'Papa—'

'What does he say about all this?' he persisted. 'Has he offered to marry you yet?'

'No, he hasn't. And even if he had I wouldn't want to. Women don't have to do that these days if they don't want to.'

'Please don't tell me what women ''want''!' he snapped. 'Maybe your own wishes should not be paramount—you have a baby to think of, in case you have forgotten!' There was a pause. 'Put Paulo on.'

'Paulo?'

'Is he there?'

'Yes, he's here.' Wordlessly, she handed the phone to the man who towered over her, but whose body language was so distant that he might as well have been a million miles away.

She stayed exactly where she was, because this wasn't what you could ever term a private conversation. She had every right to hear what they were saying about her.

'Luis?' Paulo kept his voice impassive, suspecting that Isabella's father would be angry at him for having kept her secret for so long.

'Paulo, how could you do this?'

'I'm sorry, Luis,' he said, genuinely contrite.

'A little late in the day for that, surely?' asked the older man, then sighed. 'I should have *realised* what was happening. Everyone else seemed to.' There was a moment's silence. 'Maybe it was inevitable—she always worshipped the ground you walked on—'

'Luis—' said Paulo, as alarm bells began to ring inside his head. But the older man sounded as if he was in therapy—talking through a problem in an effort to solve it.

'Maybe it was fate. I'm her father and even I thought you looked good together.' Another sigh, heavier this time. 'Still, these recriminations won't help now. These things happen in the old and the modern world. You're together now and that's all that matters. But I need a little time to get used to the idea. You understand. The last thing Bella needs at a time like this are harsh words. Tell her I'll call in a day or so, will you?'

'Sure,' said Paulo evenly.

'Goodbye, Paulo.'

'Goodbye, Luis.'

He replaced the receiver very slowly, and stood looking at it for a moment. And when he raised his head, his eyes were filled with a cold fire which sent a tremor of apprehension shivering its way down her spine.

'What is it?' she whispered.

'Sit down,' he said.

'Paulo?'

'Sit down,' he repeated.

She slid into the chair he was indicating, placing her knees together like a schoolgirl in a class photo. Which was a bit how she felt. 'OK. I'm sitting.' There was an air of seriousness about him that she had never seen there before and her heart picked up a beat. She braced herself for the worst. 'What did he say?'

He stared at her. The way she had lifted her chin— the slightly defiant gesture not quite hiding the very real fear and confusion which lurked at the back of the amber eyes. He guessed there was no easy way to tell her.

'Paulo—*what did he say*?'

He laughed, still reeling from the irony himself. 'That I am the father of your baby.'

There was a moment of disbelief, followed by a stunned silence. 'But that's crazy!' she said, shaking her head in furious denial. 'Crazy! I've never heard anything so—'

'Isabella,' he interrupted, seeming to choose his words with enough care to bring them slamming home to her. 'Just think about it.' He slid into the chair opposite hers, so that their knees were almost touching and even in the midst of her jumbled thoughts, her body still registered his proximity.

'I am thinking about it!' It was the most bizarre thing she had ever heard. How could she be pregnant by a man she had never even kissed? 'I mean, we haven't even…even…' Her words faded away to an embarrassed whisper.

'Had sex?' he supplied brutally, quashing the guilty thought that indeed they had not…just in the fevered bed of his imagination and maybe it was about time he started turning fantasy into reality. 'No, we haven't. How very right you are, Bella,' he murmured. 'It's a sickener, isn't it—to be blamed for something you haven't actually done?'

'So how can he possibly believe it to be true?'

'He isn't the only one, is he?' he snapped. 'That Stafford woman thought I was responsible. So did the doctor. Even Jessie secretly believes it—no matter how much I deny it!'

'But why?'

'I believe it's called circumstantial evidence,' he clipped out. He moved his face closer to hers, his voice low and urgent. 'Point one—you have steadfastly refused to reveal the true father's identity.'

'But—'

'Point two,' he interrupted coldly. 'As soon as you found out you were pregnant, you left Brazil and came rushing straight to England—to *me*. Didn't you?'

'Well, what if I did?' she croaked. 'That on its own doesn't make *you* the most likely candidate, does it?'

His smile was forced. 'On its own, no—it doesn't. But add that to the fact that your father noticed a certain frisson between the two of us, back in February. A chemistry which was apparently remarked on by most of the people there at the time.' He paused, and frowned, because this was puzzling *him*. 'Which was almost *nine months ago*.'

The final damning piece of evidence fell into place and made the whole picture clearer—except that it was not the true picture at all, merely an illusion. 'Oh, my God!'

'Precisely,' he snapped, and his face grew hard. 'Now I'm not going to deny the attraction which fizzed up between us, because only a self-deluding fool would do that.' His mouth twisted in tandem with the convoluted line of his thoughts. 'But nothing more than wishful thinking happened on my part. I did not have sex with *anyone* during my trip to Brazil. I can't speak for you, of course.'

She couldn't look at him, her gaze falling miserably to her lap. She knew what his eyes would accuse her of. That she had lusted after him, but had fallen into the bed of someone else almost immediately. And when it boiled down to it—wasn't that the awful truth?

'Now, the facts may be stacked up against me, *querida*—but just in case your father comes after me with a shotgun in his hand I want you to tell me one thing.'

She knew what his question would be, even before his lips had started to coldly frame the words. A question she had evaded for so long now that evasion had become almost second nature.

'Just who *is* the father of your baby?'

CHAPTER SEVEN

ISABELLA swallowed. 'His name is R-Roberto.'

Paulo's eyes grew stony as he heard her voice tremble over the name. He shook his head. 'Not good enough. I need more than that.'

It didn't even occur to her to object to that snapped demand. She was in too deep now to deny him anything. 'His name is Roberto Bonino and he—'

'Who is he?'

This was the difficult bit. 'I knew him at university.' She swallowed.

Paulo's stiffened as he recognised evasion on a mega-scale. 'Another student, you mean?'

She felt her neck grow hot. 'No.'

'Tell me, Bella.'

Something in his voice compelled her to look up at him and she knew that her pink, guilty cheeks gave her away at once. 'He…he was one of the lecturers, actually.'

There was a long, dangerous pause. 'One of the *lecturers*?'

'Y-yes.'

Somehow he had been expecting the worst, but the truth was no less devasting in its delivery. He felt the cold, dead taste of disappointment in his mouth. And the slow burn of anger. 'But that's a complete abuse of power!' he snarled.

'He was only temporary—'

'And you think that makes what he did acceptable?'

She shook her head, its weight pressing down like a heavy rock on her neck. 'No. Of course I don't.'

The anger inside him gathered and grew into bitter accusation. 'So was it love, Bella? True love? The kind that fairy-tales are made of? Eyes across a crowded room and wham-bam—' his black eyes glittered '—you're in so deep you can't think straight?'

She heard the cynicism which stained his words, and shook her head. There had only ever been one man who had had that effect on her and he was sitting within touching distance. 'No.'

He wanted to grab hold of her and lever her up into his arms, but he forced himself to stay sitting. 'What, then? What exactly *was* the relationship between you? Tell me what happened!'

Still she couldn't look him in the eye—unable to face his condemnation and scorn when she told him what lay behind her ugly seduction. That it had been Paulo who had set her senses on fire. Paulo who had set in place a fevered longing that meant she hadn't been able to think straight. It had been Paulo who had planted the rampant seeds of desire—but had left just before the inevitable harvest…

'I used to go to his psychology lectures,' she explained painfully.

'Psychology? Oh, *great*!' He felt like punching his fist through the wall. 'Do you think he'd ever thought about studying his *own* behaviour?'

She carried on as if he hadn't interrupted, a slight desperation touching her words now. 'He was more a friend than anything. At least—that's what I thought. We used to go out in a big group sometimes—'

'Didn't he have any friends his own age?' he asked sarcastically.

'Actually, he wasn't much older than most of the people he used to teach, so he fitted in.'

'Yeah, he sure did,' he agreed pointedly, then found her answering blush too painful to contemplate. 'And?' he prompted, but the harsh note of accusation had all but gone.

Isabella looked at him—at the carved perfection of his face with its intriguing blend of light and shade. A proud, beautiful face which now wore an icy-cold mask of disapproval. 'I guess I was all mixed up.' That much was true. She had been longing for Paulo—obsessed by his memory.

'And randy?' he questioned cruelly. 'Surely you're not forgetting that?'

She swallowed down a lump of distaste. 'Let's just say I wasn't completely indifferent—' She saw him jerk his head back as if she had struck him, and tried to be as honest with him as possible. 'We'd both had a few drinks and...' Her voice tailed off, too embarrassed to continue.

Paulo seethed with a terrible kind of rage. He bit the words out as if they were bitter poison while his fist itched to connect with her tutor's pretty, young face. 'You mean he got you *drunk*?'

'No, of course he didn't!' She nearly asked him what he took her for, but she didn't dare. He might just tell her. 'I had a couple of glasses of wine on an empty stomach and I'm not used to alcohol.' She looked him straight in the eye then, challenging him to condemn her. 'So go on, Paulo—call me a tramp! Call me whatever names you want, if it makes you feel better.'

Impossibly, and appallingly, he thought of what *would* make him feel better—and it had something to do with covering the soft, rosy tremble of her mouth with his.

Covering it so that the memory of Roberto's kiss would be as stale as ashes in her mind. He shook his head. 'You're no tramp, Bella,' he said softly. She had told him most of what he needed to know—so why the defensive tightening of her shoulders? 'But there's still something you're not telling me, isn't there?'

She bit her lip and looked away. 'There's quite a lot, actually. But I didn't think you'd want to know.'

His mouth hardened, unprepared for the sudden blitz of bitterness. 'I don't mean every sordid detail of your night with this...this...' He stopped himself from spitting out the only word which was halfway suitable, and one which he would never use in front of a woman. Especially about the man who had fathered her child.

'Were you a virgin?' he asked suddenly, though deep-down he knew what her answer would be.

'I... Yes.' She hung her head as he made a sound as though she had hit him. 'Yes, I was.'

Swallowing down the taste of bitter jealousy, he let his hand reach out to cup her face, his dark eyes luminous with a kind of poignant sadness.

'It should have been me,' he said softly.

Meeting his gaze, she was already close to tears, but she held them at bay for long enough to whisper, 'Wh-what should?'

He let his hand fall, so that it was on a level with her belly and then, intimately, shockingly—he reached out a finger and drew it meticulously down over the drum-tight swell of the baby and Bella gasped aloud as he touched her.

'This. This baby of yours. It could have been me, couldn't it?' he questioned huskily, beginning to stroke a tiny circle around her navel. *'This.'* And his finger undulated over her belly as the baby moved beneath it. 'Mine.'

'Yours? How could it possibly be yours?'

'How do you think? By the *traditional* method of fathering children, of course. I should have made love to you,' he whispered, but he saw that beneath the fine olive complexion, her face looked almost bloodless in response. He let the anger go for a moment and let regret take its place—a bitter, lasting regret that he hadn't felt since his wife had died.

He could barely bring himself to acknowledge the precious gift he had refused—only to have someone else step in and steal it in his place. 'If only I hadn't listened to my crazy, *stupid* conscience!' he groaned aloud.

She stared at him in confusion. 'What are you talking about?'

'Oh, Bella—you know what I'm talking about!' His words sounded urgent and bitter, but his hand felt unbelievably gentle and she let him leave it right where it was, splayed almost possessively over the bump of the baby. 'You wanted me as much as I wanted you, didn't you?' he questioned softly.

She couldn't escape the question burning from his black eyes, even if she had wanted to. And she was through with evasion and half-truths. She would not tell him a lie. She couldn't. Not now, not after everything he had done for her. Was doing for her. Even now. 'Yes,' she said quietly.

'So subdued,' he murmured. 'So unlike the Bella I know.'

She wondered if the Bella he knew existed any more, but by then the moment for sensible debate had vanished and the unbelievable was happening instead. Paulo was pulling her to her to her feet and into the warm circle of his arms and the thoughtful look on his face gave her the courage to ask, 'So why didn't you?'

It was almost scary that he knew exactly what she meant. 'Make love to you?' He stroked her thickened waist reflectively. 'How many reasons would you like? Because you were only twenty and I suspected that you were innocent, as well as being the daughter of my host?' Or because he recognised the danger she represented, as well as the excitement? A danger to his well-ordered life and its carefully compartmentalised emotions.

'Of course,' and he paused—a slow, dangerous beat. 'None of those obstacles have any relevance any more, do they?'

With a thundering heart Isabella stared at the darkening of his eyes and the deepening colour which highlighted the broad sweep of his cheekbones. And just for that moment it was easy to pretend that he really *was* her lover.

'Paulo!' she gasped, because the baby chose just that moment to kick her very hard beneath her heart, or maybe that was just the effect he had on her.

'What is it, *querida*?' His voice was gentle but he didn't wait for an answer, just bent his head and began to kiss her. And all sane thoughts dissolved as Isabella was left with the sensation of a long-awaited dream being fulfilled.

This had been too long in coming, Paulo thought with an edge of desperation as he lowered his mouth onto hers. He could not recall a hunger of such keen, bright intensity. Nor kissing a woman so heavily pregnant with such raw passion before. For a brief, heady moment he allowed himself the sensation of melting, of their mouths

moulding together as though they had always been
joined with such perfect chemistry.

But this was *Bella* he was kissing. Sweet, stubborn
Bella. And a very pregnant Bella, too. He reached his
hand out—supposedly to push her away—but the hand
somehow connected with enchanting accuracy over the
heavy swell of her breast. And he gave into temptation.
Cupped it. Kneaded it. Fondled it until he felt it peak
like iron against his fingertips and he heard her half-
moaned response.

Bella felt her knees threaten to give way. Her heart
was fluttering and so was the baby—while all the time
she could feel the heavy pulsing of desire as it began its
slow inexorable throb. She clung onto his broad shoulders and kissed him back as though her life depended
on it. And maybe it did.

He dragged his mouth away from hers with an effort
and gazed down into her flushed, dazed face. He could
barely speak, he was so aroused—so much for his rep-
utation as the cool, controlled lover! 'We have to stop
this right now, Bella,' he told her huskily. 'Jessie will
be back soon.' And so, he remembered in horror, so
would his son.

'And Eddie!' She echoed his thoughts as she franti-
cally smoothed the palms of her hands over her hot
cheeks, aware that her hair must be mussed up, her lips
stained dark by the pressure of his mouth. 'I'd better go
and…tidy myself up,' she gulped.

She made to move away, but he caught hold of her
hand, his eyes boring into her as he understood one more
reason why she had borne her secret for so long. 'That's
why you couldn't bring yourself to tell your father about
the baby, isn't it? Because this man—Roberto—abused
his position.'

She nodded, causing even more disarray to her hair. 'That's how Papa would see it, yes. He would create a big scene. Can you imagine? He might even attempt to prosecute, and then it would be in all the papers. Can't you understand why I ran to England, Paulo?'

'Yes, I can.' He nodded his head slowly. 'But you've compromised me now, haven't you, *querida*? Your father is convinced that I have sired your baby. And to tell him otherwise would risk the kind of commotion you're so anxious to avoid—even if you were willing to do so.'

'So what do I do?'

His eyes glittered as he considered her question, the memory of her kiss still sweet on his mouth. 'You stay here. With me. And Eduardo. And after the baby is born, well, then...' He shrugged as he gave his rare and sexy smile—thinking that she could work *that* one out for herself.

The arrogance and complacency of that smile brought Isabella crashing back into the real world. 'Then what?' she questioned slowly. 'What exactly are you suggesting?'

'Why, then we could enjoy our mutual passion, Bella,' he purred, seeing the darkening in her eyes and feeling his body's answering leap in response. 'After all, why should I take all of the responsibility of impending paternity, but with none of the corresponding pleasure? Live here. With me. And we will become lovers.'

Lovers.

There was silence in the room, save for the ominous ticking of a clock she had never noticed before. And, while he must know how much she wanted him, something held her back.

Because she'd already made one big mistake in her life—she certainly did not intend making another. And if she allowed herself to fall eagerly into his bed on the strength of that coolly impassive suggestion, then how would he ever have any other image of her than that of a passive sensualist, all vulnerable and needy where men were concerned?

'And just how long did you have in mind?' she questioned acidly. 'Until you've taken your fill of me, I suppose?'

He stared deep into the amber eyes, respecting the guts it must have taken to ask that question. A trace of the old Isabella, he thought—her spirit remarkably uncrushed, despite what fate had thrown at her.

'Who can say, *querida*? Until it is spent. All burned out. Until you decide where you want to settle with your baby. Who knows for how long? I certainly can't tell you.' He paused, watching carefully for her reaction. 'But of course there are alternatives open to you if the idea doesn't appeal.'

She opened her mouth to speak, but the ringing of the front doorbell shattered the spell and he moved away from her. Her eyes followed him as he moved across the room.

He was wearing only a simple sweater with a pair of faded denims. The washed-out green of the sweater only drew attention to the spectacular darkness of his Latin American colouring, while the jeans were moulded to buttocks and thighs so powerful that... She found herself imagining seeing him, every bit of him, naked and warm in the act of loving.

'Oh, yes.' He nodded, his voice deepening as he observed her flushed reaction and her darkening eyes. 'I can see that it *does* appeal.'

Pride made her tilt her chin to stare at him, but pride also made her speak from the heart. 'I can't deny the attraction between us either,' she said slowly. 'But soon I'll have a baby to think about, as well as myself. I can't just leap into an affair with you. I might feel differently after the birth.'

'You might not,' he objected.

Her eyes mocked him. 'Well, you'll just have to wait and see, won't you, Paulo?'

It was not what he had wanted to hear. Nor expected to hear. Isabella could tell that much from the frozen look of disbelief which briefly hardened his outrageously gorgeous face.

But she kept watching him, waiting for the inevitable thaw—and when it came the frustration had been replaced by an emotion he used to swamp her with, but one which had been absent just lately.

It was called respect.

CHAPTER EIGHT

'WHAT'S the matter?' Paulo flicked off the television programme he had been half-heartedly trying to watch and stared instead at Isabella, who'd been shifting her position rather distractedly on the sofa, distracting him in the bargain, despite all his good intentions.

She'd told him that he would have to wait and see and he was going to abide by her decision. Even if the effort half-killed him.

Isabella stifled a yawn as she met the soft question in his eyes, aware that he'd been sitting watching her for the best part of an hour while pretending to watch TV. She'd spent the early part of the evening having Eddie teach her a computer game and now she was paying the price for having sat upright in front of a small screen for over an hour. She shifted around on the sofa again. 'Nothing.'

'Something,' he contradicted, thinking how pale her face looked and wondering if her nights had been as short of sleep as his had. Probably not. She probably slept smug and sound in her bed, knowing that she had him right where she wanted him—dangling on the end of a string.

He sighed, realising that he'd forgotten the last time a woman had said no to him, and the last person he'd ever imagined it would be was Isabella—not after the way she'd come to such swift, passionate life in his arms. 'Come on, Bella,' he urged softly. 'I can tell you're uncomfortable.'

'Her back hurts,' explained Eddie, who chose that moment to wander into the room in his pyjamas to say goodnight. 'It always does at this time of the night, doesn't it, Bella? 'Specially if she sits still.'

'Oh, really?' Paulo shot her a look which bordered on the accusing before rising to his feet to take his son to bed to read him a story. And when he came back he found that she had changed position on the sofa, but still with that same faint frown creasing her brow.

He sat down beside her, registering the way her body tensed as his weight sank onto the sofa beside her and he slowly and deliberately stretched his long legs in front of him, smug himself now to realise she wasn't entirely immune to him. 'So how come my son knows more about your current state of health than I do?'

She shrugged her shoulders uncomfortably, aware of the arrogantly muscular thrust of his thighs. Was he lying in that provocative position on *purpose*? she wondered agitatedly. 'He heard me telling Jessie that I get backache.'

Paulo frowned, badly wanting to reach out and trace the sweet, curving outline of her lips. 'And is that unusual?' he asked huskily.

'No, it's perfectly normal. They told us to expect it.'

'Who are ''they''?' he asked softly.

'The childbirth classes I went to when I was au pairing. And the books say so, too.'

'Maybe I should read them, too,' he mused, before asking. 'Is there any known cure?'

Not for the ache in her heart, no. Backache was an altogether simpler matter. A smile hovered on her mouth in spite of the fact that her whole world seemed to be a maelstrom of swirling emotions. 'Massage,' she told him stolidly. 'It helps but it doesn't cure.'

'Hmm.' He shifted in his seat. 'Turn around, then.'

Oh, sure—having Paulo caressing her skin was exactly what she *didn't* need. 'No, honestly—'

'Turn around,' he repeated quietly. Because at least if she turned away she wouldn't be able to read the hunger in his eyes.

With difficulty she did as he said, wondering if he had noticed the slow flush of colour which had risen in her cheeks.

He moved his thumbs into the hollow at the base of the spine and heard her expel a soft breath as he began to press away some of the tension.

It was crazy—more than crazy—but this innocent act of kneading her flesh felt like the most indecent act he had ever performed. 'Is that—' his voice deepened '—good?'

Any minute now and her thundering heart would burst right out of her chest. 'It's…fine,' she managed.

Paulo's nerves were stretched to the breaking point in an exquisite state of frustration. He wondered what she would do if he slid his hands round to cup her breasts, then sighed. Because he was essentially a man of honour. And that, he thought, would be taking advantage. Definitely.

'Better?' he murmured.

'Mmm. A hundred times.' She was torn between longing for him to continue and yearning for him to stop.

'Get yourself to bed then, and I'll bring you something warm to drink.'

She shook her head. 'I'm not thirsty.'

'It's a very expensive, very delicious chocolatey drink which I went out of my way to buy you when I was coming back from work,' he coaxed, and injected a stern note into his voice. 'Because chocolate is what you told me you'd been craving, Miss Fernandes—and because I notice you just pushed your supper around your plate this evening.'

'Does nothing escape your notice?' she teased.

Very little, he thought as he steadied her on his arm. And nothing whatsoever to do with her. She looked like a different woman since coming to live with him. Pregnancy had made her hair shine like mahogany and her skin gleam with radiant, glowing health.

In her bedroom, Isabella struggled out of her clothes and into the nightshirt which made her look like a vast, white tent, and was sitting up in bed when Paulo brought her a cup of chocolate.

He sat leaning moodily on the window-ledge while he looked around the room—noticing that she must have been out into the garden and picked a selection of berried twigs and brightly coloured pieces of foliage and placed them in a tall, silver vase. Jessie never did that kind of stuff. And he liked it, he realised... He liked it a lot.

In the corner of the room stood her bag, all packed for hospital, and beside it a small pile of Babygros as well as a yellow teddy-bear which he had picked up personally after they had had to cut short their visit to the toy-shop.

'You're all ready, then?' he asked.

She followed the direction of his gaze and nodded, not missing the warm approval in his voice. 'More than I was before.'

'You were heavily into denial,' he observed slowly, remembering how she hadn't brought a single baby thing back with her that day he had picked her up at the Staffords'. 'So what changed all that?'

'Telling my father, I guess.' She sighed, and knew

that once again she owed him her gratitude. Did being indebted to the man mean she could never be his equal? she wondered. 'You were right to push me into it, Paulo. I feel such a fool now for not having the courage to do so in the first place.'

'We're all allowed to be cowards sometimes, Bella,' he said softly, thinking that if she had done that then she would never have arrived here, seeking his help. Would never have slotted into his life like this—disrupting it, yes, undoubtedly, but making it seem more *alive* than it had done for a long time. And he realised too, that her life had not been easy since she had found out about the baby. Not easy at all.

He kept his voice casual. 'How would you like to catch a taxi into the city, and meet me after work tomorrow night? I could show you my office—we could maybe grab a bite to eat.'

She looked down at her bump, horrified. 'Like *this*?'

He smiled and shrugged. 'Why not?'

'What will your colleagues think?'

He gave the smile of a man who had never pandered to other people's opinions. 'Who cares what they think?' He raised his dark brows. 'So, would you?'

'Well, I would,' she admitted, almost shyly.

In the end, she took Eddie along with her because having Paulo's son accompany her seemed to legitimise her presence. She met most of Paulo's frankly curious colleagues, seeing from their expressions just what deductions they were making about her role in their director's life.

While Eddie was busy changing the screensaver on his father's computer, she took Paulo aside and hissed into his ear, 'You do *know* what everyone's thinking?'

'That I'm such a super-stud?' he mocked.

Her eyes widened and she met the look in his eyes and started to giggle. Well, if Paulo didn't care, then she certainly wasn't going to waste her time worrying about what was, in fact, her private fantasy!

So she settled back and allowed herself to be steered through the building with all the exaggerated courtesy which would naturally be afforded to a rich man's pregnant mistress.

They toured the impressive glass-fronted skyscraper, and then the three of them got a cab to Covent Garden for hamburgers and milkshakes—or rather Paulo and Eddie ate the hamburgers while Isabella indulged herself with a very thick strawberry milkshake.

On the way home, Paulo turned to her in the taxi. 'Tired?'

She shook her head. 'Not a bit.'

'Back hurting?'

She smiled. 'My back is fine.'

He tapped the connecting glass and asked the driver to drive down around by the Houses of Parliament so that they could see the historic buildings lit up by night.

Eddie turned to Isabella. 'What an amazing night!' he exclaimed. 'It's just like being on holiday!'

Yes, it was. But holidays always came to an end, she reminded herself.

The following evening—just by way of saying thank you—she had a martini waiting for Paulo when he arrived back from work, and if he was unsettled by the distinctly *wifely* gesture, he didn't say so.

He sipped it with pleasure and regarded her with thoughtful eyes. 'Oh, by the way, a letter arrived for you from Brazil this morning,' he said, putting his drink down on the table and fishing a flimsy blue air-mail envelope from the breast pocket of his suit jacket.

Isabella stared at it. 'It's from my father.'

'I know it is. Why don't you e-mail each other? Eddie says he gave you a crash-course the other day.'

'I told you. Papa hates technology. He'd use pigeon-post if it was reliable enough.'

He smiled. 'Oh.'

She held it in her hand for a moment. She had had several conversations with her father since the one when he had slammed the paternity accusation at Paulo. She had been expecting his anger to be ongoing, but there had been none. More a kind of quiet resignation. Most unlike her father, she thought.

'Well, go on, then—open it.'

He watched while she ripped the envelope open with suddenly nervous fingers and quickly scanned the page, relief lightening her face as her eyes skated over the main portion.

'Good news?' he queried.

'*Kind* of,' she answered cautiously, but then she began to study it in more detail and her colour heightened.

Paulo was watching her closely. 'Want to read it out loud?'

'Not really.'

'Bella,' he said warningly. 'I thought we were through with secrets?'

She made one last helpless attempt at evasion. Or was it pride? 'A woman should always keep a little something back—didn't you know?'

He held his hand out for the letter. 'Please.'

She handed it over.

Paulo scanned the sheet for the source of what had

obviously made her react like that and it didn't take him long to find it.

Obviously, I would have preferred for this to happen in a more conventional manner, but I cannot pretend that I am displeased. Paulo is a fine man and a fine father. I could not have wished for a better husband for you, Bella—so cherish him well.

Paulo looked up to find her attention firmly fixed on the glass of mango juice she had poured herself.

'Bella? Look at me!'

'I don't want to discuss it,' she said fiercely, but she raised her head to meet the accusation sparking from his eyes.

'Well, I *do*! Perhaps you've already booked the church and arranged the venue?'

'I have not!'

'But we're getting married—apparently—so don't you think the prospective groom should be informed?'

'Do you honestly think I told my father we were getting married?'

'How should I know?' he questioned arrogantly, thinking that he would like to untie that velvet ribbon in her hair and have it tumble all the way down her back. Her naked back. '*Now* where are you going?'

She jerked the chair back from the table, her breath coming in short little gasps. 'As far away from you as possible!'

He was on his feet in seconds, standing in front of her and forming a very effective barrier. 'Stop it and calm down.'

'I do not *feel* like calming down!' she told him distractedly. 'I feel like...like... Ow, ow, *ouch*!'

'Is it the baby?' he demanded immediately.

It felt like someone tightening a piece of string around her middle and then tightening it again. Her hands reached up and she clutched onto his shoulders, her nails digging into him. 'I don't *think* so!'

'I'm going to call the doctor—'

'No! No. Wait a minute!' She panted and paused. 'No, that's OK. I think it's gone.'

He dipped his head so that their eyes were on a level. 'Sure?'

Her heart seemed to suspend its beating. She was still, she realised, gripping tightly onto his shoulders. And through the thin shirt she could feel the silken yield of his flesh to the hard bone beneath. 'Qu-quite sure.'

She let her hands fall away, and Paulo forced himself not to grab them back. She was about to have a baby, for God's sake—and here he was wanting to feel her in his arms again.

'Maybe I'd better call the doctor?'

She shook her head. 'To say what?'

'That you had a pain—'

'Paulo, it was more of a twinge than a pain. And it's gone now.'

'Sure?' he demanded.

'Positive.'

'I just don't want to take any chances.'

'Who's taking any chances? The pain has gone.' She spread her arms out as if to demonstrate. 'See? All gone. I don't want to be one of those neurotic women who calls out the doctor ten times—and every time it's a false alarm. Now go away. Don't you have any work to do?'

Paulo shrugged unenthusiastically. He wanted to stay. He wanted to kiss her. He wanted to do a lot more besides. Maybe it was better if he *did* clear off. 'I've always got work to do.'

'Then go away and do it,' she shooed.

'And what will you do?'

'I'm not planning on going far. You don't have to worry.'

'I'm not worrying.' But that was a lie, he thought, as he headed off to his study. He was—and, oddly enough, his worries were not the ones he would have imagined at all. It didn't bother him one iota that most of the world imagined that he was the father of her unborn child. In fact, wasn't that a supposition he had deliberately *flaunted* by inviting her into his office last night?

No. He found himself wondering what on earth would happen when the baby arrived. He had told Bella that she had a home for as long as she wanted one and now it suddenly occurred to him that she might not want a home at all. Or to be his lover.

As she had said herself, she might feel differently after the birth. Because now that her father knew and seemed to be coming round to the idea—and bearing in mind that she could usually twist him round her little finger—then what was to stop her going back to Brazil as an unmarried mother?

He imagined her leaving with her baby, and instead of a sense of reprieve he was aware of a great yawning idea of emptiness.

When Elizabeth had died he had decided to live his life in the best way he could for their son, completely forgetting that life never remained static. That life *was* change. He frowned as he switched on the computer.

Isabella prowled the house like a thief, restless without knowing why and looking for something to do. She sat down and wrote a long and chatty letter to Charlie and Richie, as promised—and hoped that Mrs Stafford would be adult enough to pass the letter on to her two young sons.

When she had stamped the envelope, she found a feather duster and wandered from room to room, polishing flecks of dust from all the mirrors. Next she cleaned the two sinks in the downstairs cloakroom, even though they were spotless and gleaming. After she had rearranged all the spices in the store-cupboard, she rang the local Portuguese delicatessen and placed an order for a delivery.

'I'd like rib and shoulder and breast of pork, please. Sausage. Linguica. Green cabbage. Oh, and beans.'

'And when would you like this delivered, madam?'

She frowned at herself in the mirror, thinking that she looked especially enormous today. 'Any chance of tomorrow morning?'

There was no hesitation whatsoever—probably because of the delivery address, Isabella decided.

'That shouldn't be a problem, madam.'

When Eddie got in from school the next day, he came straight into the kitchen as he always did, to find Isabella up to her elbows in cooking utensils. He strolled over to the work-surface, where she was chopping onion as if her life depended on it.

'What are you doing?' he asked with interest.

'Jessie isn't here, so I'm making feijoada for our supper.' She smiled.

'What's that?'

'Come on, Eddie,' she chided. 'You remember? It's Brazil's national dish. With lots of meats and different sausages—'

Eddie looked down at all the different pots which

were cluttering the work-surface. 'Looks difficult to make.'

'Not difficult. Fiddly. Lots of different things all added to one big pot at different times. See?'

'Can I help?'

'Of course you can help. Wash your hands first and then you can prepare this garlic for me. See this clever little machine? Now—' she leaned over his shoulder '—put each bulb in here—and it will crush it up for you.'

That was where Paulo discovered them when he arrived home from work. Unknotting his tie, he wandered into the kitchen to find Isabella removing a large piece of meat from the pot with Eddie standing glued to her side.

Paulo smiled—as much at the sight of their obvious companionship as the warm, homely smell which triggered off snatches of boyhood memories. 'Mmm. Feijoada.' He sniffed, as he walked into the kitchen. 'What's brought all this on?'

'You don't like it?' she asked him anxiously.

He smiled conspiratorially at his son. 'Show me the man who doesn't like feijoada—and I'll show you a man who doesn't deserve to eat! No, I was just thinking that it's a pretty adventurous thing to cook, if you're feeling tired.'

'But I'm not feeling in the least bit tired!' She energetically threw a handful of bay leaves in the pot, as if to demonstrate.

Jet eyes lanced through her. 'So I see,' he agreed slowly. 'And wasn't that polish I could smell in the hallway?'

'Oh, it's Jessie's day off and I was just waving a duster in the air,' she explained airily. 'More for something to do than anything else.'

He nodded. 'Eddie—want to go and get changed out of your school uniform, now?'

'Sure, Papa.'

He stood looking at the image she made once Eddie had gone. Her stomach was so big that she should have looked ungainly as she moved towards the cooker—but she didn't at all. She just seemed perfectly ripe and extremely beautiful—even though her cheeks were all flushed from bending over a hot pan.

'You're nesting,' he said suddenly.

She turned round, wooden spoon in hand. 'Mmm?'

'It's called nesting. That's why you're doing all this.' He waved a hand around. 'Cleaning and polishing and chopping and cooking. You're getting ready to have your baby.'

'You can't know that.'

'Yes, I can. Elizabeth did it, too—it's nature telling you to make your home ready for the new arrival.'

She searched his face for signs of sadness. 'Does having me here like this bring it all back?' she asked softly.

He didn't look away. 'A little.' He saw the look of contrition on her face and shook his head. 'It's not a problem, Bella—I came to terms with what happened to Elizabeth a long time ago. I had to—for Eddie's sake. But—' and he narrowed his eyes into a searchlight stare as he saw her face grow pale '—it does give me the upper hand when it comes to knowing what I'm talking about. And that was another one, wasn't it?'

'Another what?'

'Contraction,' he elaborated roughly.

Suddenly an intimation of what was about to happen to her whispered fingertips of fear over her skin. She shook her head and gave the beans a stir. 'It can't be,' she said, a slight edge of desperation in her voice. 'The baby isn't due until next week.'

'And babies never come when they're supposed to.'

'Oh, really?'

'Yes, really,' he agreed calmly, when he saw her attempt to turn a grimace into a smile. 'And for goodness' sake, will you stop pretending that you're not getting contractions, when it's pretty obvious to me that you are?' he exploded.

So she wasn't fooling him at all! At least his words gave her licence to drop the wooden spoon with a clutter and to bend over and clutch at her abdomen as she had been dying to do for ages.

And it took a moment or two for her to realise that he was standing in front of her, his face a shifting complex of shadows looking for all the world like some dark guardian angel sent to protect her. Her eyes were big and fearful as she stared up at him. 'Ow,' she moaned softly. *'Ow!'*

'What is it?' he demanded, his hands spanning her expanded waist and feeling her tense beneath his touch. 'Another contraction?'

She nodded her head. His hands felt strong and real and supportive, but wasn't all that an illusion? In fact, wasn't everything just an illusion compared to the razor-sharp lash of pain she had just experienced? You spent nine months imagining that something couldn't possibly be happening, and then all of a sudden, it was. And there wasn't a thing you could do to stop it. 'Paulo—I'm scared.'

He lifted one hand from her waist to soothe softly at her head, the shiny curls clinging like vines to his fingers. 'I know you are, *querida*, but you've just got to take it easy, remember? Slow and easy. This is what you've been preparing for, Bella. You know what to do. Remember your breathing. And the relaxation—all that stuff you did in your childbirth classes—I know it too, don't forget. I've done it before. I'll be there to help you.' He paused. 'If you want me there.'

A few minutes later, she choked out a gasp at a new, sharper pain. 'Another one!'

Paulo glanced down at his watch. 'That's ten minutes,' he observed, as calmly as possible.

'Is that OK?' she whispered, because everything she had been taught seemed to have flown clean out of her head.

He frowned. This all seemed to be happening far more rapidly than it was supposed to. 'I'd better ring Jessie and get her in to come and look after Eddie,' he said, watching her body tense up again. 'I think it's time I took you to hospital.'

This time the contraction almost swamped her, and the sweat ran down in rivulets from her forehead. And if this was just a taste of things to come...

Isabella gripped Paulo's hand, not feeling the sticky moistness from where her nails dug into and broke the skin to make him bleed.

'Don't leave me, Paulo,' she moaned softly. 'Please don't leave me.'

That vulnerable little plea smashed its way right through his defences, and he was filled with an over-whelming need to protect her.

'I won't leave you,' he promised, as he reached for the telephone.

CHAPTER NINE

THE whirling blue light of the ambulance cast strange neon flashes over both their faces and the sound of the siren screamed in their ears as they sped towards the hospital.

Through a daze, Isabella gripped onto Paulo's hand, squirming around to try and get comfortable—but no position seemed to help.

Paulo was trying to stay calm, but it was harder than he had anticipated. He had tried paging Dr Cordosa, but the obstetrician had been sailing and was currently making his way back up the motorway. Paulo glanced down at Isabella, thinking that if her labour continued at this alarmingly fast rate, then Dr Cordosa would miss it anyway.

'How are you feeling?' he asked.

'Hot!' Sweat beaded her forehead. 'Will Eddie be OK?'

'Stop worrying about Eddie—he'll be fine. Jessie is there with him.'

'What about the feijoada? It's only half-cooked!'

'Bella!' he said warningly.

At the hospital they were rushed straight into the Emergency Department, where Bella was put, protesting, onto one of the trolleys. Paulo held her hand all the way up to the labour ward and when the midwife arrived to examine her she continued to grip onto it as tightly as a drowning woman.

The midwife gently pushed him aside, speaking to him as if he was a child himself.

'Can we have the father on the other side of the bed, please?'

He was about to say that he wasn't sure that he'd be around for the main part of the action, when he felt Bella's fingernails digging into the palm of his hand again. He looked down at her, the question in his eyes being answered by the beseeching look in hers. His heart pounded. When she had begged him not to leave her, she had meant it, he realised with something approaching shock.

'Sure,' he said, but he delicately kept his eyes on her face while the midwife conducted her intimate examination, and for the first time in his life he actually felt *shy*.

What Paulo wanted for Isabella more than anything was a straightforward birth, but he knew the instant that the midwife raised an expressive eyebrow at her runner across the delivery room and the runner hurriedly left the room that maybe this birth was not going to be straightforward at all.

He could tell that the team was trying to play any drama down, but he knew when two other doctors entered the room that things weren't going according to plan. He quickly read their name badges. One was an obstetrician and the other was a paediatrician. So didn't that mean that both mother *and* baby were in danger?

His heart made a painful acceleration, and he found himself praying for the first time in years. Dear God— he had already lost one woman in his life—surely fate would not be so merciless as to take the other one?

But he must not let his fear communicate itself to Bella. Not when she was being so brave. He watched the look of grim determination on her face as she conquered the rising tide of each contraction and he was reminded of her fundamental fearlessness. He gritted his teeth, frustrated at his inability to help her when she most needed him.

For Isabella nothing existed, save the powerful demands of her body—everything else faded into complete insignificance. She refused the drugs they offered her, but gulped down the gas and air, which helped. And so did Paulo, just by being there. She gripped onto his hand when the contractions grew so strong that she did not think she could bear to go through another one. Whenever she unclenched her eyes, his face swam into her line of vision and she could read the encouragement there.

And something else, too—a kind of pride and admiration which filled her with a powerful new energy.

People had started telling her to push, but she didn't need them to tell her anything, because by then the urge to get her baby into the outside world had become too strong to resist.

'Here's your baby!' called someone.

'Come and see your baby being born, Paulo,' urged one of the midwives.

Paulo couldn't have refused the midwife's request, even if he had wanted to. And he didn't. He knew that it was important for Bella to have someone witness an event which was as miraculous for her as for any other woman—even if the circumstances surrounding it *were* unconventional.

He let go of her hand and walked down the room to see the dark, downy head beginning to emerge and his heart gathered speed as a shoulder quickly followed. He was aware of furious activity executed with an unnatural calm, and then the baby slithered out, but made no sound as precious seconds ticked by. There was more activity, and then, quietly and dramatically, the first tenuous wail of life which hit him like a punch to the guts.

'It's a girl!' said the paediatrician, bending over the baby and cleaning the tiny nose and mouth.

Paulo walked over to Isabella and looked down at her pale face and the hair which was matted to her brow and cheeks. He bent down and brushed a damp curl away, so tempted to kiss her. 'Congratulations, *querida*,' he whispered instead. 'You have a beautiful daughter.'

A great wave of relief washed over her, leaving her shaky and exhausted in its wake. 'Can I hold her?'

'Just for a moment,' said the paediatrician, as he carefully placed the tiny bundle in her arms. 'Her heartbeat was a little low during the delivery and she was a little slow to breathe—so we're going to take her off to Special Care for her first night, just to keep an eye on her. Does she have a name yet?'

Bella stared down at the impossibly small head. The peep of dark curls through the swaddled blanket. And all the dark, frightened thoughts which had driven her half-crazy at the time she'd become pregnant—dissolved like magic. Because this baby *was* magic. A sense of love flooded her. 'She's called Estella,' she said, the overwhelming emotion making her breath catch in her throat. 'It means "star".'

'No, you're the star,' said Paulo softly, but he spoke in Portuguese, so that only Bella understood.

She looked up into his face and saw that his eyes were bright—the warmth and care in them surely too strong to be imagined? As proud as if he really *were* the father. Her lips began to tremble and she looked down and kissed her baby's head.

*   *   *

Bella opened her eyes in the middle of the night and wondered what was different. She sat bolt upright and looked around her. After the delivery she had submerged herself in the most delicious bath and had then fallén asleep, with Paulo sitting like some dark, beautiful guard beside her.

But now Paulo had gone and the crib by the bed remained empty. Fear clutched erratically at her heart as she reached out and rang the bell by her side and the nurse came hurrying into the room.

'Yes, dear—what is it?'

'Where's my baby, please?'

'She's still in Special Care—but not for very much longer. I spoke to them a little while ago, and she's doing just fine.'

'I want to see her.'

'And you can. But why don't you rest for the time being, and wait until the morning?'

'I want to see her,' said Bella with a stubborn new resolve in her voice she didn't recognise.

The nurse insisted on taking her up to the Special Care Unit in a wheelchair and as they drew up in front of the cubicle, Bella felt tears of relief pricking the back of her eyes as she watched the tableau being played out in front of them.

Behind the bright glass screen stood Paulo, and he was cradling the tiny baby in his arms, his lips moving as he spoke softly to her.

And Bella made a broken little sound. A primitive sound which seemed to be torn from some place deep within her.

The nurse looked down at her. 'Are you all right?'

Bella nodded. *I love him. I've always loved him.*

The nurse beamed. 'You new mothers! Of course you love him—you've just had his baby, haven't you?'

Isabella hadn't even realised that she had spoken the words out loud, but suddenly she didn't care. And maybe Paulo realised that he was being watched or spoken about, because he suddenly looked up, and his brilliant smile told her that the baby was going to be fine.

'I'm going in,' she said to the nurse.

'Let me wheel you—'

'No. I want to walk. Honestly.'

Paulo stood and watched while she climbed carefully out of the wheelchair, watched the proud way she refused the nurse's arm and held herself erect, before walking stiffly into the cubicle and over to where he held Estella.

She looked into the black brilliance dancing in his eyes—eyes as dark as Estella's—thinking that he could easily be mistaken for her baby's father. But he wasn't. And he never would be. 'You've got my baby,' she whispered.

'I know. Can't resist her. Do you want her back? I thought so. Here—' And he held her out to Bella with a soft smile. 'Go to Mummy.'

Very gently, he placed Estella into her arms. The baby instinctively began rooting for her mother's breast and Isabella felt a tug of love so powerful that she stared down at the shivering little head with an indescribable sense of wonder.

And Paulo stood outside the magic circle, watched the first tentative explorings between mother and child, appalled by the dark feelings of exclusion which ran through him.

He wanted her, he realised. Just hours after she'd had

another man's baby and he wanted her so badly that it hurt. Now what kind of person had he become?

He glanced up at the ward clock which was ticking the seconds away. It was four in the morning. 'I'd better get back home. I want to be there for Eddie waking up. I'll bring him to visit tomorrow. Goodbye, Isabella—sweet dreams.'

Suddenly he was gone, and Isabella and the nurse stared after his dark figure as he strode off down the hospital corridor without once looking back.

The nurse turned to Isabella and gave her a confused kind of smile. 'Why, the naughty man didn't even kiss you goodbye!' she clucked.

Isabella dropped a tired kiss on the top of Estella's head. 'I think the excitement of the delivery must have got to him,' she said. Far better to think that than to imagine that he hadn't kissed her because he simply hadn't wanted to…

CHAPTER TEN

THE following morning, Paulo arrived on the ward before the night-staff had gone home, bearing a bottle of champagne tied with a pink ribbon.

Three staff midwives looked up as he appeared at the office door and their mouths collectively fell open at the sight of the tall, dark-haired vision in a deep blue suit and an amber tie of pure silk.

'I know I'm early.' He smiled. 'But I wanted to see Bella before I went to work.'

The trio all sprang to their feet, smoothing down crisp white aprons. 'Let me show you where she is,' they said in unison.

Paulo's black eyes crinkled with amusement. 'I know where she is,' he said softly. 'I asked one of the nursing assistants. And I'd like to surprise her, if I may.'

Bella was busy feeding Estella, the baby nestled into the crook of Bella's arm while she tugged enthusiastically at her mother's breast. It was the strangest and most amazing sensation, Bella decided, her mouth curving into a slow smile of satisfaction.

Paulo stood outside her cubicle and watched her, marvelling at how easily and how naturally she had taken to feeding her child.

Breast-feeding had not been quite so popular when Eddie had been born and, in any case, Elizabeth's postnatal blues had meant that he had been able to take on most of the bottle-feeding so that she could rest.

He thought how the bearing of Isabella's breast,

though intimate, was not especially erotic. Then he saw her remove one elongated and rosy nipple and wondered just who he had been trying to kid.

Bella looked up to find herself caught in the intense dazzle of his black eyes and she felt the tremble of her lips as she gazed across the room at him.

And any idea that she might feel differently after the birth or that her words of love yesterday had been the hormone-fuelled fantasies of a post-partum woman were instantly banished. Because just the sight of his dear, handsome face was enough to engulf her with an unbearable sense of yearning.

He came in and put the champagne down on the locker. 'Hi,' he murmured.

'Hi,' she said back, feeling almost shy—but maybe that wasn't so very surprising. He had seen her at her most exposed—body and emotions stripped bare as she had brought new life into the world.

'I thought I'd pop in on my way in to work.'

And play havoc with her blood pressure in that beautifully cut dark suit. She smiled. 'I'm glad you did.'

He looked down at the baby who had now flopped into an instant, contented sleep. Had Eddie ever been that tiny? he wondered in bemusement. 'How is she?'

'Beautiful.'

Like her mother, he thought. 'Can I take her—or would that disturb her?'

She shook her head. 'Take away,' she said huskily.

He bent to pluck the swaddled bundle from her arms, surprised at the pleasure it gave him to hold Estella again. She smelt of milk—and of Bella—and he felt compelled by a powerful need to drop a kiss on top of the tiny head.

Isabella watched while he cradled and kissed Estella,

and in that moment she loved him even more for his warmth and his generosity. *I wish he would hold me like that,* she thought with fierce longing.

'I phoned your father,' he said.

Her heart thudded a little. 'And?'

'He's puffed up with pride—I never imagined that he could go a full minute without saying anything!'

No need to tell her that he had then uncomfortably submitted to Luis's congratulations and endured the inevitable questions about who the child most resembled—Paulo or Bella. 'It's difficult to say,' he had replied smoothly, without stopping to question why the evasion had slipped so easily from his lips.

'How's Eddie?' she asked.

He stroked the downy head with the tip of his nose. 'Excited. More than excited—even the computer doesn't have an edge on this baby. I'll bring him in with me tonight.'

Paulo visited her morning and evening until she and the baby were discharged a week later, and he had an air of anticipation about him as he led her outside to where a large and shining family car awaited them.

With her arms full of blanket-swathed baby, Isabella blinked at the gleaming motor in surprise. 'What's this—a new car?'

'That's right.' He opened the door for her. 'Like it?'

'It's lovely, but what happened to the old one?'

'Nothing. It's in the garage—this is an extra. We need a bigger car now that there's four of us.'

He doesn't mean it the way it sounded, she told herself fiercely, as she bent to strap Estella into the newly installed car-seat.

Eddie was standing on the doorstep waiting to greet

them, and he was hopping up and down with excitement. His father had taken him most days to visit them in hospital, leaving Paulo and Isabella feeling distinctly invisible! All Eddie's attention had been fixed on the tiny infant who clung so tightly to his finger with one little fist.

Paulo had found the experience strangely moving, noticing the interaction between his son and the new baby with something approaching remorse. He had always been so certain that Eddie should be the exclusive child in his life—always steeling himself against committing to a relationship again and the possibility of more children. Not that it had ever been a hardship. No woman had remotely tempted him to do otherwise.

But it was sobering to see how his son behaved with the baby—as if someone had just turned a light on inside him. As baby paraphernalia began to be delivered to the house, Paulo found himself wondering whether an immaculate house with a working father and a housekeeper was not vastly inferior to the noise and mess and love which this new addition seemed to have brought with her.

Isabella brought the baby into the house, walking with exaggerated care and still feeling slightly disorientated. She had only been away for a few days and yet she was returning as a different person. As a mother. With all the responsibilities which went with that role. Yet the sense of unreality which had descended on her since the birth had not completely left her, even though Estella was real and beautiful enough.

It was hard to believe now that Paulo had actually held her hand throughout. He had seen her stripped of all dignity—moaning and writhing with pain. He had wiped her brow just before she pushed the baby out and he had even watched her do *that*. But he had not touched her, nor kissed her and somehow she had thought—no, hoped—that he would. Maybe *he* was the one who had changed his mind.

But her troubled thoughts disappeared the moment she looked around her. The hallway was festooned with balloons and a lavish arrangement of scented pink flowers was standing next to the telephone. From the direction of the kitchen drifted a sweet, familiar smell.

'It's the feijoada,' explained Paulo as he saw her sniff the air and frown. 'We froze the meal you were making when you went into labour. Eddie said it would be perfect as a welcome-home feast.'

'Eddie's right—it's the very best,' said Isabella, looking at a silver and pink balloon saying 'It's a Girl!', which was floating up the stairs. 'And this all looks wonderful, too.' Her voice softened. 'You must have worked very hard.'

Jessie came out of the kitchen, a wide smile of welcome on her face. 'Welcome home!' she said, and hugged her.

'Thank you, Jessie!'

'Can I have a little peep?'

Isabella pulled the cashmere blanket away from the miniature face and sighed. 'Isn't she beautiful?''

Paulo found himself looking at the mother instead of the baby. There was no doubt that she looked absolutely breathtaking—her figure seemed to have gone from bulk to newly slender almost overnight. The nurse had said that because she was so young and fit her body had just sprung back into shape straight away.

She was wearing a pair of saffron-yellow jeans and a scarlet shirt stretched tight over her milk-full breasts. The abundance of copper-brown curls were tied back from her face with a black ribbon and her unmade-up face looked dewy and radiant.

So what was the matter with her?

She seemed so distant, he thought. Detached. Her movements jerky and self-conscious—her only true warmth appearing when she was relating to the baby. Or to Eddie. But certainly not to him.

'Come upstairs and see what we've done for Estella,' he said softly.

'Can I hold the baby for a bit?' said Jessie eagerly. 'Give you a bit of a break?'

'Of course you can!' smiled Isabella but, with the infant out of her arms, she felt curiously bereft.

'Let me see her too, Jessie!' said Eddie.

Isabella's heart was in her mouth as Paulo followed her up the stairs. 'Where exactly are we going?' she asked him.

'The room right next door to yours,' he said, a faint frown appearing as he heard the unmistakable note of wariness in her voice.

But Isabella's nerves were temporarily forgotten when she opened the door and looked inside and saw what a lot of effort he must have gone to. 'Oh, my goodness,' she sighed. 'How on earth have you managed to do all this?'

It was the cutest baby's room imaginable.

One wall was dominated by a mural of Alice in Wonderland—complete with white rabbit and grinning Cheshire cat—while the rest of the walls were the exact colour of cherryade. An old-fashioned crib stood next to the wall, with flounces of lace nestling delicately amidst the pink gingham, while a rag-doll sat with several of her sisters on the gleaming, newly painted window ledge.

She found herself thinking that he had gone to an awful lot of trouble for a stay which might only be temporary and her heart gave a sudden great lurch of hope.

'Like it?' he asked.

She turned to him. '*Like* it? Oh, Paulo—who in their right mind could not help loving it?'

'And are you in your right mind?' he asked her softly.

Something in his tone made the hope die an uncertain death. 'I…think so. Why do you ask?'

He smiled, but there was a cold edge to his voice. 'You are wearing the kind of expression which I imagine the early Christians might have adopted just before being fed to the lions,' he said drily. 'What's the matter, Isabella—did you think I was planning to drag you up here to make love to you already?'

From the look on his face, the idea clearly appalled him. 'I didn't say that,' she said woodenly. She trusted him not to hurt her, to respect her and not to leap on her before she was ready—yet he was hurting her far more by standing on the opposite side of the room like some dark, remote stranger.

He frowned at the reproachful look in her amber eyes. 'Bella, you're tired. And you've just had a baby. What kind of a monster do you think I am?'

'You're not a monster at all,' she said. 'I'm just grateful for all the trouble you've gone to—'

Damn it—he didn't want her *gratitude*, just some sign, some indication that she still wanted him. 'Don't mention it,' he put in coolly.

Rather desperately, she said, 'But it must have cost a lot of money?'

The light went out in his eyes. 'Please don't mention it again, Bella. Let's just call it a small repayment for the kindness shown to me by your father all these years.'

And wasn't that a bit like saying that the debt was now repaid? She wondered?

She wanted to touch him, to run her fingertips along the hard, proud outline of his jaw, but inside she was scared.

She *had* just had a baby and she also had a poor track record where men were concerned. If she started a relationship with Paulo, she had to be very sure that she was doing the right thing. And while in her heart there wasn't a single doubt, she needed him to know that she wasn't acting on a whim when they made love.

If he still wanted *her*—and she needed to be sure of that, too.

Paulo saw the discomfiture on her face and wondered if she felt compromised. 'Of course, you mustn't feel that just because I've had the room decorated you have to stay.' His eyes were full of question. 'You may have already made your mind up that you want to leave.'

She wondered if she was keeping her horror carefully concealed. 'Leave?'

He forced himself to continue, even though the words nearly choked him. She had to have a let-out clause, he decided grimly.

'You might want to go home,' he suggested softly. 'To Brazil. You could take Estella and show her to her father.'

She met the dark challenge in his eyes without flinching. 'But Roberto doesn't want me; I told you that. And I don't want him! It's over—it never really began.' Because he had only ever been a shadowy lover—an unwitting replacement for the only man she had ever really wanted.

'But he might feel differently once he knows about the baby.'

'He isn't going to *know* about the baby!'

'And don't you think he has a right?'

'I think I have a right to choose whether or not to tell him,' she told him softly.

'But your feelings towards him may change,' he argued, wondering what contrary demon was making him put forward a case which was detrimental to what *he* wanted. 'What if Estella grows to resemble her real father more and more—what then? You might find the biological tie irresistible—you might even want him back again.'

She didn't react—would not let him see how much his callous words had hurt her. He'd sounded as though that was what he *wanted* her to do. Maybe, as a father himself, he was now becoming indignant on Roberto's behalf.

She heard the sound of Estella's cry floating up the stairs towards her and in an instant she had stilled, lifting her head to listen. 'Is that Estella?'

'Yeah. Saved by the baby!' He noticed that there were two small, damp circles of milk on her shirt and gave a wry smile, which did little to ease the ache in his groin. 'But mightn't it be best if you change your shirt before you go down?'

She looked down her damp and rocky nipples and when she lifted her head to meet his eyes, she saw the unmistakable spark of desire. And laughter. 'Just go, Paulo!' she said huskily.

Downstairs he found Eddie sitting on one of the vast, overstuffed sofas, cradling the baby expertly in his arms.

'Are you OK holding her?' Paulo asked gently, and the look his son gave him cut him to the marrow.

'Of course I'm OK! Oh, Dad, look! She's so cute! Loads of the other boys in my class have got baby brothers or sisters—I wish Estella could be *my* little sister! Why can't you marry Isabella, and then she can?'

'Because real life isn't like that,' he said gently.

'Well, real life sucks!'

'Eddie!' Paulo opened his mouth to issue a short but terse lecture on the unattractiveness of swearing, but something in his son's haunted expression drew him up short.

He had lost his mother so young that he had no real memory of her, Paulo remembered painfully. Maybe it wasn't so surprising that Eddie had already forged a bond with this fatherless little infant, Paulo thought, and felt a lump catch in his throat.

The sense of loss had been with him for a long time— long after the pain of bereavement had gone. The random cruelty of life had made him wary of committing to anyone again—but now he was beginning to realise that you couldn't live your life thinking 'what if?'. He had once accused Isabella of cowardice, but hadn't he been guilty of emotional cowardice himself?

'Can I take her for a minute, son?' he said gently.

When Isabella came back downstairs, with her hair flowing loose around her shoulders, it was to find father and son being extremely territorial with *her* baby! She looked over at the two males sitting up close on the sofa, their dark heads bent over the sleeping bundle. To an outsider, she realised wistfully, they would look exactly like a normal family.

'Can I use the phone, Paulo?'

'You don't have to ask every time,' he growled.

'Thank you.' She gave him a serene smile. 'It's just that I'd better ring my father and tell him I'm safely out of hospital.'

'And neither do you have to tell me the name of everybody you're calling.'

'I'll remember that,' she said gravely.

Paulo paced up and down with Estella locked against his neck, desperately trying not to succumb to the temptation of eavesdropping into her conversation.

Maybe their conversation of earlier had been closer to the mark than he had imagined. Maybe even now she was talking to her father about the possibility of returning to Brazil... He had brought the subject up and she had grown quiet long enough to suggest that she had given it some serious thought. And why *shouldn't* she feel differently now? That was what babies tended to do to you.

'Paulo?'

He looked up to see those delicious curls falling almost to her waist and his lips tingled with the need to kiss her.

'You got through OK?' he asked thickly.

She nodded, thinking how tiny the baby looked in his arms. And how right. 'He said to thank you for the photos, and asked how the hell did you get them over to him so quickly?'

'There isn't much point me having access to all the latest technology—' he shrugged, with a smile '—unless I'm actually going to use it. What else did he say?'

'He's desperately excited. Buying up every pink article in Salvador. And...'

He narrowed his eyes. 'And what?'

Isabella hesitated, glancing over at Eddie and Paulo guessed that she wanted to speak to him in private.

He followed her out into the hallway. 'What is it?' he demanded softly.

She met his eyes with embarrassment. 'Well, since we haven't issued a denial—' she paused again.

'Go on,' he prompted.

She shrugged awkwardly. 'He still seems to be labouring under the illusion that we're getting married.'

'Oh, does he?' asked Paulo slowly.

'I really should tell him that we aren't, but...'

He looked up, trying to work out what emotion was colouring her voice. 'But what?'

She sighed. Paulo did not need to know that her father thought he was the most wonderful thing since sliced bread. And that the prospect of his only daughter making such a glorious marriage seemed to have erased the memory of her unconventional pregnancy. 'Oh, I don't know,' she hedged. 'It seems to be keeping him happy.'

'Then why don't we keep it that way?' he suggested thoughtfully.

CHAPTER ELEVEN

ISABELLA turned Estella's night-light on and went quietly downstairs to the dining room where Paulo was waiting for her.

He looked up as she came in, his dark face thoughtful as she did up the final button of her bodice, and he sighed. How in God's name had he ever been stupid enough to think that breast-feeding a baby wasn't erotic?

'Is she asleep?' he asked.

'Out for the count.' She slid into her seat and watched while he heaped a pile of glossy black grapes into the centre of the cheeseboard, thinking that Saturday night dinner in the Dantas household was an experience not to be missed.

Because, despite the undeniable masculinity of his appearance, she had discovered that Paulo was no slouch when it came to finding his way round a kitchen. And that, as well as a hundred different ways with pasta, he cooked a mean steak. But then, as he had told her, Jessie might have been around to do the bulk of the house-keeping duties—but she certainly wasn't on call twenty-four hours a day, seven days a week!

He was sitting staring at her now, the black eyes softly luminous. 'So what did the midwife say?'

Isabella swirled red wine around the globe of her glass and pretended to study it. She certainly wasn't going to repeat the midwife's brisk question word for word! 'Sex-life back to normal by now, I expect?' And Isabella had nodded her head vigorously, because how—*how*—could she possibly tell the nurse the truth? That she had never, ever been made love to by Paulo Dantas. But that oh, she wanted to.

'Hmm, Bella?' he prompted on a murmur.

'Oh, just that Estella was the most beautiful, bouncing baby—'

'Uh-huh. Anything else?'

'And that we're doing everything right.' She heard the word 'we' slip off her tongue and silently cursed it. Just because she continued to play happy families inside her head, that didn't mean the rest of the world had to join in. Even though Paulo seemed to be doing a masterly job of playing happy families himself.

'That's all?'

Isabella put her glass down on the table. 'Paulo, just what are you trying to say?'

He suspected that she knew damned well. 'Nothing.'

'Look, why don't you come right out and ask me?'

'It would shock you, pretty lady.' He gave a gritty smile, thinking that lately she didn't look just pretty—she looked absolutely knock-out beautiful. Like tonight, for instance—in that silky red thing which covered her from neck to knee and yet left absolutely nothing to the imagination. He wondered whether it had been designed for the sole purpose of having a man itching to tear the damned thing off.

'I told you.' She sipped her wine and smiled encouragingly at him. 'I'm unshockable, these days.'

Paulo pushed his untouched plate of cheese aside and stared at her, thinking that much more of this and he was going to go out of his mind. Because, even though he and Bella and Eddie and Estella had been living the kind of lifestyle which usually featured in the glossy supplements of Sunday newspapers, deep down, the undercur-

rent of tension between the two of them had been unbearable.

There had been all the frustration of having her so
close—but not close enough. Of nights laced with hot,
erotic dreams which left him waking up, sweat-sheened
and frustrated—despite the inevitable conclusion to
those dreams. Of knowing—or hoping—that she was lying there tossing and turning, just the same as he was.
Aching with the need to touch her, to lay his hands on
a body which was driving him slowly insane. So that
going to work each morning had become a welcome
kind of escape from the unwitting spell she was casting
over him.

She moved with such unconscious grace that he found
he had never enjoyed watching a woman quite as much
as he did Isabella. There was nothing of the flirt or the
tease about her. She was as uncomplicated in her young,
strong beauty as any of the thoroughbreds he had seen
her ride on her father's ranch.

But a deal was a deal and he forced himself to remember the stark facts. He was older—and far more
experienced. He knew just what to do and exactly which
buttons to press if he wanted to get Bella into his bed.
But the decision had to be hers, and hers alone. And,
whilst before the baby had been born he had deliberately
flirted with her, he no longer trusted himself to do that.

A distended stomach meant that you couldn't exactly
throw a woman to the floor and make love to her like
there was no tomorrow. Which was what he had felt like
doing earlier when Isabella decided that she was going
to dress up for dinner. He swallowed down a mouthful
of wine without really tasting it.

Isabella stared at him through the candles, willing him
to say something—*anything*—which would bring the

subject round to the question of them becoming lovers without her having to actually blurt it out.

'Paulo?' she whispered huskily, her eyes full of question.

'Yes, *querida*?' He kept his voice neutral and his smile bland.

She stared at him in frozen disbelief. Because when push came to shove she needed a little more in the way of wooing. She knew he had promised her nothing other than an affair which would 'burn itself out', and she could accept that. She wasn't asking him to sign the register and produce a band of gold—just give her some sign that he really, really *wanted* her—because she was damned if she was going to beg!

She slammed her napkin down onto the table before jumping to her feet. 'Oh! Paulo Dantas!' she cried frustratedly. 'You are so…so…'

'So?' he goaded, his black eyes laughing even while his body sprang into aching life.

'Stupid!'

And she pushed her chair back and walked straight out of the dining room, resisting the urge to slam the door behind her—because Eddie was in bed, fast asleep, and so was Estella.

She got as far as the top landing before she heard the sound of soft footfalls behind her, and for some reason the idea that he was silently chasing her through the house was unbearably exciting. She speeded up until she was almost past his bedroom door, when a hand appeared from behind to grab her wrist and to twist her round to face him and she nearly fainted with pleasure when she saw the hunger written darkly in his eyes.

'Stupid, you say?' he drawled softly.

Her heart pumped erratically. 'D-did I?'

'Stupid?' He gave a low, exultant laugh. 'Let's see, shall we, *querida*?' And he pulled her into his bedroom and softly kicked the door shut behind them.

Isabella felt the instant shimmer of arousal as his arms locked tightly around her waist and he stared down at her, his eyes devouring her with a hot, dark fire.

'Oh, *querida*,' he said, on a low groan of submission before giving in to the temptation which had been eating away at him for too long now. 'Bella, *querida*.' He felt like a man who had strayed into paradise unawares as he crushed his mouth down on hers, feeling the rose-petal softness of her lips. He kissed her until he had no breath left and then he raised his head. 'Do you want me?' he asked dazedly.

I've always wanted you. 'Yes,' came her throaty response as she wrapped her arms around his neck and clung onto him like she was drowning and Paulo represented safe harbour. Her gorgeous, beautiful Paulo. 'Yes, yes, yes.'

Paulo couldn't remember a kiss this hot or this intense and he knew that if she continued to generously press her body against him like that, that he would end up taking her against the wall. And he didn't want to just ruck her dress up and push aside her panties, ending up with his trousers round his ankles while he thrust long and hard and deep into her. He groaned.

Well, he did—of course he did. But she deserved more than that.

'Come here,' he said breathlessly. 'Come to bed.'

She was barely aware of the sumptuous fittings. Or the vast bed with its cover of rich, earthy colours. All she could see was the intense black light shining from his eyes as he sat her down, and began to unbutton the bodice of her dress.

'I want to touch you,' he said shakily. 'I need to touch you. Every bit of you. Inside and out.'

Bella shivered, unable to look away, feeling the buds of her breasts begin to tighten and the honey rush of desire as it soaked through her panties. She wondered if he could see the love which must surely be blazing from her eyes, but maybe she had better keep them closed. Love wasn't part of the deal, was it?

Paulo's fingers faltered for a moment as he caught an unmistakable scent of her sex, but he forced himself to continue unbuttoning, even though he would have willingly bought her twenty replacements if only he could rip it off. Her fingers had started to flutter over the silk of his shirt, skittering downwards in a way that made him shake his head.

'No,' he whispered.

'No?' She wanted to be good for him. She wanted to give him pleasure and she had read that all men liked to be touched *there*.

'*Querida,*' he said, speaking with difficulty because he felt seconds away from exploding. 'I've been wanting this for too long.' Because if she touched him there…

He peeled away the dress and a moan of rapture was torn from his lips. Her breasts were as full as they had been during her pregnancy, and very, very beautiful. He dipped his head reverentially towards one, and flicked the tip of his tongue towards one hardened nipple which pushed pinkly through the gossamer-fine black lace.

It was like being injected with some earth-shattering drug and Isabella fell helplessly back against the mattress, her hips moving in synchrony with her disbelieving gasp of pleasure. 'Please, Paulo,' she whispered, though she had no real idea what she was asking him for.

The husky plea and erotic action threatened to end everything before it had started and Paulo groaned again. He forced his head away from its sensual plundering of her lips, staring down into amber eyes which now looked black as raisins.

'Easy,' he breathed raggedly. 'For God's sake, Bella—take...it...easy.'

She wondered how she was supposed to do that. Especially now that his hand was slithering up her skirt, and then he gave a disbelieving little moan.

'Wh-what is it?' she stumbled.

'Stockings.' He swallowed. 'You're wearing *stockings.*'

Isabella heard the deepening of his voice and smiled. She might just be a girl from a ranch in the middle of nowhere, but there were some things that every woman over the world should know.

'Doesn't *every* woman wear stockings?' she asked him innocently.

'They should.' He groaned again. 'They should.'

But then his fingertips had moved beyond her suspenders to the cool, pale flesh of her thighs. And beyond. Oh! 'Paulo!' she breathed. '*Gato. Querido gato.*'

'You are making this bloody difficult for me,' he groaned as her head fell back and she moved distractedly again. Unable to resist, he briefly touched the warm, damp silk of her panties until he remembered that he was trying to undress her. His fingers skated away and she mouthed a silent prayer of protest, so that one finger in particular came skimming back again.

He could feel her fullness and her wetness and tightness, heard the broken words which escaped from her lips and which made no sense to him. She spoke in a mixture of English and Portuguese, her voice heavy with longing and thick with need.

He gave up and began to touch her with rhythm and purpose, thinking that this wasn't how it was supposed to happen.

Well, maybe part of it was. Hadn't he dreamed of seeing her like this, her body stretched out with abandon on his bed? Writhing with need and with desire and no thought of anything other than pleasure—the wild tumble of her hair painting his pillow with such dark curls.

He gave a small smile as he rubbed his finger against her and she nearly leapt off the bed. He had expected passion, yes. And response, yes—that, too. But this…

He dipped his head down and took the blunt tip of her nipple into his mouth, while his finger continued to tease and play against her.

Isabella felt like she had entered another world—a world dominated by sensation. By pleasure. By Paulo. And he seemed to know exactly what to do to make it get better all the time…

With something approaching astonishment, he felt her begin to tighten with an incredible tension, which could only mean one thing and he stared down into her face. Saw the mindless seeking of rapture which made her oblivious to everything except what was just about to happen in her own body. He speeded up the rhythm and spoke to her in her own language, sweet, erotic words he had never used before, words which made her melt enchantingly against his finger.

'Paulo!' she called out, and the slurred pleasure in her voice was tinged with surprise.

He smiled as he saw the sudden, frantic arching of her back, the incredulous little gasp she made as she reached that elusive, perfect place and then began the slow, shuddering journey back to sanity.

He watched the gradual stilling of her body, the flush which crept and bloomed like a flower on her neck. The way her lips parted in a helpless little sigh. The slumberous and languid stretch, like an indolent cat in front of a fire. And then the thick fluttering of her lashes as her slitted eyes gazed up at him.

'*Oh,*' she breathed uninhibitedly. 'What was *that*?'

He had suspected. No, deep down he had known. But her question—with all its implications—filled him with such a heady sense of his own power that it was as much as he could do not to throw his dark head back and give a loud, exultant laugh.

So. Roberto had given her a baby, yes. But no pleasure.

'*That, querida* of mine,' he purred, 'was the pleasure you deserve. The pleasure I intend to give you…over and over and over again.'

'*Again?*' She swallowed, with a greedy gulp.

He smiled. 'As many times as you like. But for God's sake let's get these clothes off.' His smile became rueful. He really *was* going to have to take control here, or he would never manage to get her—or himself—into bed!

And he wanted to. Needed to. Needed to feel close to her, skin on skin. Limb on limb.

He found the side fastening of her dress and slid the zip down—sliding the silky garment down over the curve of her hips with a hand which shook like a schoolboy's. And it was a long time since he had undressed a woman like this.

Those who had been in his bed since Elizabeth's death had all been icons of experience. So eager. So orderly. Neatly disappearing into the bathroom before returning to bed, all washed and toothbrushed and douched, smelling of perfume and soap and chemicals.

While Bella... She smelt like a real woman. He bent his head to unclip a stocking and again caught the raw perfume of her sex as it drifted towards him, and he resisted the urge to bury his head in the dark blur of curls which was lying with tantalising temptation above the creamy flesh of her thighs.

Later, he thought. They could do all that and more— but later. He dropped the dress onto the floor, and the stockings and garter belt followed, until she was just lying there in her bra and panties.

Her breasts were swollen, pushing against the black lace of the bra she wore and he found himself praying that she wouldn't have to go and feed the baby. But then he remembered that she had slipped away at the end of dinner, and he gave a great shuddering sigh of relief. Now, how selfish is *that*? he asked himself, as he tugged the lace panties down over her knees, trying hard not to touch her—anywhere—because he was holding onto his self-control only by the thinnest possible thread.

'Get into bed,' he said urgently.

'Touch me again,' she begged him, but he shook his head.

It had been too long. He had wanted her for too long. 'If I touch you again, I'll explode,' he husked, and the expression in his eyes made her draw in a shivering breath of excitement. 'Get into bed while I get undressed.'

She watched him take his clothes off. His face was shadowed in the unlit room as first the white T-shirt was removed to reveal the quietly-gleaming olive of his muscular torso. The black jeans followed, sliding them down over the powerful shaft of his thighs until he stood in just a pair of dark silk boxer shorts. His movements were naturally slinky and sensual as he peeled off the final piece of clothing.

Isabella's eyes widened. *'Gato,'* she murmured out loud, without thinking, and his smile was one of pure brilliance.

He paused only to tear open a condom and to carefully sheath himself with it and Isabella wondered if it was normal for a man to be that aroused, that quickly.

He drew back the cover and climbed into bed with her, pulling her into his arms, and smoothing the rampant curls away from her face. 'I don't know very much,' she admitted huskily.

'I'll teach you everything I know,' he promised and felt her shiver with anticipation in his arms. Her eyes were as bright as stars and the flush on her neck was beginning to fade. He bent and kissed the tip of her nose, just for the hell of it. And then her lips. A soft, sweet, drugging kiss that went on and on until he could wait no longer.

He pushed her back against the pillow and lay over her, his elbows taking all his weight, while the creamy swell of her breasts pushed alluringly towards him.

'Scared?' he asked.

She opened her eyes very wide. 'Why should I be scared?'

'It's your first time since having a baby. I'll be very—' he swallowed, feeling unbearably moved by the look of trust in her eyes '—gentle.'

Her faith in him was implicit. She felt the moist tip of him pushing against her and she gave an experimental little thrust of her hips, so that he nudged gently inside, filling her completely. And if she shuddered, then so did he. 'Be what you want to be, Paulo.'

He gave up. The questions could come later. Right now, it was her turn. And his. His.

He made one long, slow, hard stroke. And then another. Dipping his head to kiss her, his tongue copying the same, slick and erotic rhythm. Increasing the tempo as her control began to leave her. Watching the opening of her lips in a frozen exclamation as it started happening to her all over again.

And he could no longer wait. Nothing in the world could have stopped him. Nothing. He tensed and steeled himself, aware that this was going to feel like nothing had ever felt before.

And it did.

Oh, it did.

CHAPTER TWELVE

PAULO opened his eyes to find his head resting on the glorious cushion of Isabella's breasts. And that she was trying to slip out from underneath him. He tightened his arms around her. 'Oh, no,' he objected sleepily. 'You're not going anywhere.'

'Paulo,' she whispered. 'I must. I hear Estella and I need to go and feed her.'

He rolled onto his side, and snapped the light on, blinking at the sudden intrusion, but just in time to watch her climbing out of bed, beautifully and unashamedly naked.

'You'll come back?' he asked.

Isabella pulled the red dress over her head, not bothering with underwear. The front fastening of the dress meant that she would easily be able to feed the baby, and then she had better take a shower and...

She shook her head. 'I'd better not—it's two in the morning.'

He propped himself up on his elbow, and the black eyes glittered by the lamplight as he watched her. 'So?'

'By the time I've fed her, and changed her and settled her back down for what's left of the night—there won't really be time for me to come back in here.'

If he had learnt one thing and one thing only during that exquisite interlude, it was that she liked him to talk dirty.

'But I haven't finished with you yet,' he said quite deliberately.

Isabella swallowed as she heard the dark resolve in his voice, but knew that she had other responsibilities than being his lover. She was a parent, too. And so was he.

She bent to pick her disgarded panties and bra from the carpet and looked him straight in the eye. 'I don't think I should be here when Eddie wakes up.'

'You won't be! His room is right along the corridor and he's the world's heaviest sleeper—you know that,' he objected. 'Besides, I always wake first.'

'What if for once he doesn't?'

'He always knocks first.'

'But *we* might oversleep,' she told him softly, thinking that if they carried on the way they had been doing up until half an hour ago they might risk oversleeping for a week!

'Then I'll set the alarm.'

'Paulo!'

'OK, OK.' He sat up in bed and raked his hand back through the thick, dark hair, knowing deep down that she was right, damn her—and yet oddly irritated by her determination. Because at that moment he wanted her so badly that he felt like he would have shifted heaven and earth to have her back here in his bed.

Isabella smoothed her hair down and blew him a kiss. 'Bye.'

'Come over here and kiss me properly.'

'Or?'

He laughed, but the laugh was tinged with sexual danger. 'Guess?'

Her heart thundered in response as she walked over to the bed and bent down over him and he was given a tantalising glimpse of the shadowed cleft between her breasts. Her face and then her mouth hovered into his line of vision and she pressed a sweet, swift kiss on his lips, before going back to the door.

He very nearly said, When will I see you?

Until he remembered that he could see her whenever he wanted. Mmm. He sighed and smiled and snuggled into the pillow and was asleep in seconds.

Feeling hot and sticky and more than a little uncomfortable, Isabella fed Estella, changed her and then sang gently to her for a little while.

In her arms the baby snuffled, oblivious to the ever changing play of emotions on her mother's face. Isabella put her down in the beautiful gingham crib, tucked her in and stood looking down at her for a long moment. She thought about the years to come——God willing—— when she would gaze down at her daughter like this.

She jammed her fist in her mouth and turned away, tears burning at her eyes as she realised just how irrevocable the sexual act could be. Out of her desperate attempt to put Paulo out of her mind had come this tiny baby.

And tonight. Irrevocable for a different reason— though there would be no baby. Paulo had made sure of that.

She thought about his tenderness and his passion. The way it had really seemed to be *her* that he wanted in his bed. Not just because she was a body, and any body would do.

Tonight had been irrevocable because it had sealed the truth in her heart once and for all. That she loved this man Paulo Dantas. Would love him forever. And that made her more than vulnerable where he was concerned.

He had been totally honest with her. He had told her she could stay with him for as long as... What had he said? 'Until it is spent. All burnt out.' Just as he had told her that they should indulge their mutual passion.

Well, now they had. So what came next?

One thing was for sure, she decided, peeling off the scarlet dress and dropping it into the laundry basket. She needed to keep some vestige of independence—if only to prove to herself that she didn't need him around every minute of every day. Because if that happened she would be lost.

The last thing she wanted was to become totally dependent on Paulo—to become addicted to his beautiful, strong body and his quick, clever mind.

Because everyone knew how difficult addictions were to kick. It was better to never get started in the first place.

Isabella woke for Estella's early-morning feed and then took a long, long shower, arriving in the dining room for breakfast at the same time as Eddie.

'Hi, sweetheart,' she smiled.

'Hi, Bella. Where's Estella?'

'Guess?'

'Sleeping!' he grinned.

'You've got it in one! You can go in and say goodbye to her before you go to school, if you want.' She saw the warmth on his young face. 'Tell you what—when you get home tonight, you can help me to bath her. Would you like that?'

'Oh, Bella—*can* I?'

'Can you what?' asked a deep, sleepy voice, and Isabella's mouth dried as Paulo walked into the dining-room.

'Hi, Papa! Isabella said I can help bath Estella tonight!'

'That's nice,' said Paulo blandly and, sitting down opposite her, poured himself a glass of juice and raised it up to her in a silent, sexy toast.

Isabella struggled to hold onto her self-possession, but it wasn't easy. What did he think he was playing at? Usually he presented himself for his morning bread and fruit already dressed for work. Wearing an immaculate suit, a pristine shirt and a silk tie which made him look like a walking advertisement for executive-hunk.

So *why* was he barefoot and unshaven, wearing a faded old T-shirt—having just thrown on *the same pair of jeans that he had worn last night*? And now a bare foot had moved underneath the table and was inching its way suggestively up her leg!

She snatched it away as if it had been contaminated and thought about pouring herself a cup of coffee, except that her hand was shaking so much she didn't think she would be able to make the cup connect with her mouth.

She met the glittering jet of his gaze. 'Won't you be late, Paulo?' she asked him pointedly.

'Late?' he enquired sunnily. 'I'm a director of the bank, *querida*. I can stroll in late once in a while if I feel like it.'

'But Dad.' Eddie frowned. 'You told me that if you're a director you must always set an example—and that you should only ever be late if you've got a genuine reason to be. Like that time when I didn't want to go in because we had a maths test, but you made me.'

'He does have a point, Paulo.'

'Oh, *does* he?' He glared dangerously, and then, drawing in a breath, managed to smile. 'Anyway,' he said casually, 'I thought I'd work from home today.'

Isabella knew exactly what he was playing at—and she wasn't going to let him do this. It was vital to her sanity not to let him invade every waking moment of her day as well as her night.

'Oh, what a pity I won't be here.' She smiled.

The glower deepened. 'What do you mean, you won't be here?'

'Just that I'm taking Estella to see the doctor.'

He stared at her. 'What's the matter with her?'

'Nothing.' Her mouth softened. 'It's just a regular check-up.'

'Well, he can come here—I thought we agreed that!'

'No, we did not!' she said quietly. 'That was before—when I was pregnant and exhausted. I *need* to get out, Paulo—and Estella needs the fresh air, too, because it's good for little babies. Right?'

The black stare iced through her. 'Right,' he said coldly.

She only toyed with a croissant and, in the end, gave up and went to the utility room to find a clean sheet. She was just tucking it into the base of the pram when she heard Paulo come up behind her. She was prepared for him to touch her, but he didn't—what she was not prepared for was the irritation which was sending dangerous jet sparks glittering from his eyes when she turned to face him.

'What's the matter, *querida*?' he purred, thinking that he had never been so expertly turned down by a woman before. And that as a method of increasing desire it was proving achingly effective. 'Been having second thoughts this morning?'

'No, of course not.'

'Then why are you so intent on keeping me at arm's length?'

Isabella looked over his shoulder to check that no one

else was around. '*Jessie's* here!' she hissed. 'What do you expect?'

He shrugged. 'So I'll give her the day off.'

'No!'

'Yes—'

'What, so *you* take the day off and then give Jessie the day off—and you and I spend the rest of it in bed together, I suppose?'

He grinned. 'Sounds pretty good to me.'

'Well, I don't think it's a good idea—in fact, I think it's the worst idea I've ever heard!' Well, maybe that was overstating her case a little, but she needed to make him understand how she felt.

There was a long, dangerous pause. 'Would you care to explain why?'

Isabella sighed, because this wasn't easy. She wanted him—she wanted him too much, that was the problem. 'Paulo, I desperately need to maintain some sort of routine with my baby, not launch headlong into a sizzling new love-affair with you.'

'Surely the two aren't mutually exclusive?'

'No, of course they're not... But I think it's important that I'm there for Estella. If she were *our* baby we'd both be gazing at her non-stop, not each other—'

'But she's not *our* baby,' he pointed out, unprepared for a sudden great lurch of sadness.

'No, she's not. That's why I need to get to *know* her—we need to bond—and if I'm in your bed all the time, then we won't.' She looked at him with appeal darkening the huge, amber eyes. 'You know we won't.'

Paulo sighed. The irony was that he wouldn't have it any other way. If she'd ignored the baby while playing all kinds of erotic sex-games with him, then he would have found it a complete turn-off.

'No, I guess you're right.' He sighed again. 'But night-times…and I mean *every* night-time…those are our times.' He gave her a look of dark, shivering intent. 'Got that?'

'Oh, yes.' She swallowed, and reached out her hand to touch his face, but he stopped the movement instantly, handcuffing her wrist between his thumb and forefinger while he shook his head.

'Oh, no, Bella,' he said softly. 'You can't have it every which way. You can't just love me and leave me, then kiss me goodbye and leave me aching all day.' And he swiftly covered her mouth with a sweet, hard kiss which sent *her* senses reeling, before giving a devastating and glittering smile as she gazed up at him in dismay. 'See? It hurts, doesn't it, sweet *querida*?'

But, before her befuddled brain could begin to think of an answer, he had turned on his heel and left.

By the evening Paulo had calmed down a little, though he conceded that his buoyant mood might have had something to do with his anticipation of the night to come.

On the way home from the bank, he stopped off at the florist and bought an extravagant display of white, scented flowers—'nothing too *obvious*', he had told the florist, who had taken one look at him and suggested red roses—plus chocolates and a video for Eddie.

He arrived home to find the house strangely silent. Eddie was sitting in the study, laboriously doing his homework, and Isabella was sitting by the fire in the smaller sitting room, breastfeeding the baby.

She hadn't heard him come in and carried on, blissfully unaware of his presence by the door, murmuring sweet nothings to the child who suckled her, and he felt a sudden great urge to kiss her.

Instead he said softly, 'Hi!'

She looked up and her heart leapt with the sheer pleasure of seeing him. 'Hi.'

'Good day?'

'Sort of.' She hesitated. 'Paulo—about this morning—'

'I'm sorry—'

'No, I'm sorry—'

'I said it first,' he teased softly, and produced the lavish bunch of flowers from behind his back like a magician magicking a rabbit out of a hat.

'For me?'

'Well, who else?'

She buried her nose in the blooms and breathed their scent in. 'Jessie?'

'No, seriously.'

'Paulo, I *am* being serious. She's—'

'Where is she?' He sniffed the air. Yes, *that* was the odd thing. Normally when he arrived home from work, Jessie was crashing around in the kitchen, cooking something for supper. But tonight there were no tempting aromas to signal the arrival of an imminent supper. 'Where is she?' he repeated.

'She's gone out to buy champagne.'

He frowned. 'But we've got plenty of champagne in the house.'

'I know we have. But she wanted it to be *her* champagne. *Her* treat.'

'*Querida*, you aren't making much sense.'

'Paulo—' She drew a deep breath. 'Jessie's gone and got herself engaged!'

'Jessie has?' He shook his head. 'I don't believe it!'

'Well, you'd better. It's true. In fact, that sounds like the door—so why don't you ask her yourself?'

In the distance, the front door slammed and Jessie came breathlessly into the room, carrying a brown paper bag with a foil-topped bottle in it, smiling so much that her face looked fit to burst.

'Jessie, is this true?' he asked, mock-sternly. 'Are you about to take the plunge and get married?'

'Yes,' Jessie beamed. 'It's true! Isn't it wonderful?'

'I guess it is,' he said slowly. 'It's just come as a bit of a shock, that's all.'

'It was a shock to *me* when Simon proposed,' confessed Jessie. 'I mean, we haven't *really* known each other for that long, and...' She gave a self-conscious and slightly apologetic shrug. 'He wants me to stop work as soon as you'll let me. You won't be needing me for much longer, anyway, will you?'

Paulo started, wondering what was happening to the smooth and well-oiled machinery of his life. 'You're not *leaving*?' he demanded, aghast.

Jessie frowned at him. 'Well, of course I'm leaving,' she told him softly. 'I can't keep coming in twice a day to cook your meals when I have a husband of my own to care for, can I? And besides—' she shot a quick smile at Isabella '—I sort of got the idea that I was becoming supernumerary around here anyway. You won't miss *me*, Paulo—not any more. You've got Isabella and the baby here now.'

Paulo opened his mouth to say something, but thought better of it. Now was not the time to selfishly think about his own needs and Jessie had been indispensable to him. She had helped and supported him through all these years—so now he must be genuinely happy for her.

'Congratulations, Jessie,' he smiled. He held out his arms to her and gave her an emotional bear-hug.

Over the top of her head, he tried to catch Isabella's eyes, but all her attention seemed to be concentrated fiercely on the baby in her arms. 'We'd better get that champagne opened and order in some pizza,' he observed thoughtfully. 'Let's make it a party!'

Supper was served amidst much excitement and some chaos in the dining room, where Simon was telephoned by Jessie and summoned in to join them. The tall librarian was clearly nuts about his future bride, and Isabella felt a pang of emotion which felt appallingly close to jealousy. But she fixed a bright smile onto her lips as they all raised their glasses in a toast, even Eddie.

It was late by the time that the newly engaged pair left, giggling like a couple of teenagers, while Eddie was yawning again and again.

'Come on, son,' said Paulo softly, as he shut the front door. 'Bed.'

'G'night, Isabella,' yawned Eddie.

'Goodnight, sweetheart.'

She felt oddly nervous as she busied herself throwing away the half-chewed slices of pizza and tipping the dregs of champagne down the sink, especially when she turned to find Paulo standing watching her.

'Leave that,' he said tersely.

'But—'

'*Leave* it, I said.' His voice roughened. 'And for God's sake just come over here and kiss me, before I go out of my mind.'

She didn't need to be asked twice. She went straight into his arms and raised her face tremulously to his, before he blotted out everything but pleasure with the pressure of his lips.

He raised her face to look at him, his brows criss-crossing as he took in the faint blue shadows beneath her eyes. 'You're tired,' he accused softly.

'Are you surprised?' She smiled.

He shook his head, feeling the instant spring of arousal as he thought about what had happened. 'No. I was pretty rampant with you last night—I couldn't keep my hands off you.'

'I noticed,' she murmured. 'Did you hear me complaining?'

'Nope.' He lifted her hand to his mouth and began to gently suck at each fingertip in turn, enjoying the way her eyes darkened in response and the impatient little shake of her shoulder as she squirmed for more. 'Tonight, though, you sleep.'

She blinked up at him in alarm. She had planned to ration her time with him, yes. That was why she had sent him to work this morning. But she had saved the nights exclusively for him. Only maybe he didn't want that any more. Maybe once had been enough to slake his thirst. 'Alone, you mean?'

He gave a short laugh, as if she just suggested something obscene. 'No, with me. In my arms. But definitely no sex.' He told himself that he had resisted women in the past—women far more experienced at seduction than Bella was.

Then wondered just who he was trying to fool.

CHAPTER THIRTEEN

'ISABELLA—there's a fax just coming in for you from Paulo!'

'Coming!' Isabella tucked the blanket around Estella and switched on the musical mobile above her head. 'Thanks, Jessie,' she said, walking into the study to see Paulo's fax machine spilling out paper. 'What does it say?'

Jessie looked affronted. 'I haven't read it! It might be...personal.'

Isabella didn't reply as she leaned forward to rip the finished message off. Jessie wasn't stupid. These days, it was an open—though unacknowledged—secret that she was sharing Paulo's bed at night. A fact brought pointedly home to her when her lost necklace was produced from down the back of the mattress in his room. But at least Jessie had had the tact not to ask any questions when she had handed it back to Isabella. In fact, these days Jessie was more interested in holding her hand up to the light to study her brand-new engagement ring.

Isabella smiled at the housekeeper before reading it. 'Only a few days to go now. Paulo's going to miss you.'

Jessie shook her head. 'I don't think so. He doesn't need me any more, not really. It's time for him to move on as much as me.'

But Isabella wasn't really listening; she was too busy reading the fax. It was a copy of a newspaper cutting, written in Portuguese, and it was a birth announcement

172

taken from one of Brazil's biggest nationals. She frowned at the date. A week ago. It said:

To Isabella Fernandes and Paulo Dantas—a girl. Luis Jorge Fernandes is delighted to announce the birth of a beautiful granddaughter—Estella Maria—in London, England.

Isabella quickly crushed the paper in her hand and walked out into the hallway when the phone started ringing. She snatched it up, knowing that it would be Paulo.

It was.

'You got my fax?'

'Yes.' She chewed on her lip. People *thinking* that he was the father was one thing, but actually seeing it in print... 'I don't what to say, Paulo—my father had no right to do that. I don't know what possessed him!'

'Don't you?' came the dry response. 'I've got a pretty good idea. He's obviously trying to shame us into getting married!'

It occurred to her that he couldn't possibly have picked a more loaded or offensive word to use. '*Shame* us?'

'You know what I mean. That's how he'll see it.'

'Well, I'd better telephone him right away,' she said stiffly. 'Just to set the record straight.'

There was a pause. 'Unless you want to, of course.'

Isabella stared at the hand which was tightly gripping the receiver. 'Want to what?'

'Get married.'

As a proposal it left a lot to be desired. Even if he *did* mean it—and she couldn't be certain that this wasn't just another example of Paulo's mocking, deadpan humour. Imagine if it was, and she started gushing, yes please—forcing him to hastily back-track and tell her he'd been joking. 'I won't be blackmailed into anything,' she told him fiercely.

Another pause. 'OK, Bella. But don't ring your father until we've discussed it.'

'Paulo—'

'Not now, Bella. I'm in the office and I'm busy. It's Friday, remember? We'll talk about it when I get home.'

She put the phone down, feeling as mixed up as she'd ever been. How *dared* her father? How *dared* he? And Paulo wasn't much better, either. Idily drawling a proposal of marriage down the phone as if he were asking her whether there was any bread in the freezer, when marriage was a serious undertaking which should not be undertaken lightly! How *could* he?

She felt glad that it was the weekend, and that Eddie had gone to stay the night with a schoolfriend. The last thing she felt like doing was eating, but Jessie had made a casserole and Paulo would be hungry, so she put a low flame underneath it.

Paulo walked into the kitchen to find her stirring at the pot, thinking that she managed to look a very sexy hausfrau indeed, and was just about to tell her so, when he saw the tell-tale glitter of anger sparking from the amber eyes, and merely remarked, 'Hmm. No point asking for a kiss, then.'

Her anger was threatening to spill over like some horrible corrosive liquid, but she forced it under control. 'Correct.'

He pulled a cork from a bottle of wine, and poured himself a glass. 'Like some?'

'No, thanks,' she said tightly.

He sipped the wine, looking at her defensive body language through the thick forest of his lashes, and sighed. 'OK, Bella—just who are you angry with? Me, or your father?'

'Both of you! And I don't need any patronising proposals of marriage from *you*, Paulo Dantas! Just because Jessie is leaving and you think you'll be left in the lurch! Well, it's probably cheaper in the long run to employ another housekeeper instead of bothering to get married. It will certainly be less trouble!'

'How very right you are,' he agreed coolly, and walked out of the kitchen, leaving Isabella staring after him, feeling...feeling...well, *cheated*. She had wanted a passionate defence of his offer to marry her—not that rather bland indifference, which confirmed her worst fears that he hadn't meant it at all.

She heard him slamming out of the house without bothering to say goodbye or tell her where he was going and, for the first time since they had become lovers, Isabella slept in her own room that night. She lay wide awake, and thought she heard Paulo's door close long after midnight.

And in the long, grey hours before dawn she was able to realise with an aching certainty, just how much she missed him. She missed him lying next to her. And not just Paulo as her lover—even though he was the most perfect lover imaginable. She missed the way he held her during the night. The bits that came *after* the sex. A lazy arm locked possessively around her waist. A thigh resting indolently on hers. He made her feel warm and comfortable and very safe.

She must have dozed fitfully because, when Estella woke at six the following morning, Isabella felt more exhausted even than when she had first brought the baby home from hospital. And there seemed little point in going back to bed.

She wasted time in the shower and spent even longer getting dressed, forcing herself to make coffee and toast and thinking that the sound of movement might bring Paulo out of his bedroom. But it didn't. And she couldn't just barge in there and wake him. Could she? Even if she was sure that he would have wanted her to.

So she wrapped the baby up warmly and took her outside in the pram. The park was almost deserted and it was a bitterly cold day. The trees were all bare now, and the leaves had been neatly brushed up and taken away, leaving a stark winter landscape behind.

But Isabella didn't even register the plummeting temperature. She was trying to tell herself that maybe it was a good thing that her father had brought matters to a head. She was going to *have* to come to some kind of decision about her future. Because she knew in her heart that she couldn't just stay on indefinitely, playing pretend families with Paulo and his son.

And didn't Eddie risk getting hurt too, the more she hung around slipping irresistibly into the role of mother-substitute? What would happen to him when the relationship finally petered out?

Beneath the snug protection of bonnet and blankets, Estella began to stir and when Isabella looked at her watch she was amazed to discover that she had been out walking for almost two hours.

She went back to the house with all the enthusiasm of someone who was just about to sit an exam, and she had just bumped the pram through the front door when she heard the low sound of men's voices coming from the sitting room.

She left Estella asleep in the pram and walked into the room. Paulo stood by the golden flicker of the fire, his face as she had never seen it before. Dark and cold and frighteningly aloof. And then the identity of the other man froze itself onto her disbelieving brain.

The man stood with his back to her, his hair untidily spilling over the collar of an old denim jacket. But she recognised him in one sickening instant.

It had been almost eleven months since she'd last seen him, unshaven and loudly snoring off a hangover. She'd crept from his bed in the middle of the night, feeling that she couldn't have sunk any lower if someone had tied a heavy stone to her ankles and thrown her into the river.

But as a result of that night had come her baby—and although with hindsight she would never have chosen to behave in the way she did she could no more imagine a world without Estella than she could a world without...

'Paulo?' she whispered.

'You have a visitor,' he bit out. 'Aren't you going to say hello, Isabella?'

'Hello, Roberto,' she said flatly, but she kept her face expressionless, because some instinct told her that she was in some kind of inexplicable danger here.

Roberto turned around, and Isabella was unprepared for the revulsion which iced her skin, but still she kept her face free of emotion. She recognised now that she'd been a different woman when she had fallen for his practised seduction. That his smile was weak, not careless. And that he'd taken advantage of her vulnerability and her status as one of his students.

'What are you doing here?' she asked him quietly.

'Why don't I leave you both in peace?' put in Paulo silkily, but Isabella barely registered his words or even the fact that he had slipped silently from the room.

Because she could scarcely believe that Roberto was *here*, standing in front of her, his very presence tainting the place she had come to think of as home. 'How did you find me, Roberto?'

He shrugged. 'It wasn't difficult—thanks to your father's birth announcement. Paulo Dantas is one of Brazil's better-known bankers. And England's, too, it would seem,' he added jealously, as his eyes flickered around the room. And then it was *her* turn to be sized up, and he gave her a sly smile. 'You know, you're looking pretty good for a woman who has just had a baby—'

'Why are you here?' she asked, in a frozen voice.

'Why do you think?' He looked around him. 'Where is she, Isabella?'

Her heart pounded in her chest. 'Who?' she croaked.

'Please don't insult my intelligence.'

She opened her mouth to tell him that he flattered himself, but shut it again. Making him angry wasn't a clever idea.

'Where is she?' he repeated. 'My daughter. Estella.'

At the sound of Estella's name on *his* lips, Isabella grew rigid with terror, but she did her best to hide her reaction, instinctively knowing that she must appear strong. She must. 'You've only just arrived, Roberto,' she said softly. 'And have had nothing to drink. Let me offer you a little something.'

She saw him hesitate, and saw greed win out over the question of paternity—despite the earliness of the hour.

'Yeah, a drink would be good. Dantas could barely bring himself to speak to me without spitting.' His eyes glistened as they watched the uneven rise and fall of her breasts. 'But I guess I know why.'

'I'll go and get you that drink,' she breathed, and she just about made it to the kitchen before crumpling into a chair, her fingers jammed between her teeth to prevent herself from crying out in real terror.

And that was how Paulo found her. He didn't say a word until she raised her head to look at him, and what he read in her eyes caused him to flinch.

But he needed to hear it from her.

'Do you want him?' he asked flatly.

She swallowed down the nausea. 'How can you even ask?'

He forced the words out. 'Because he's the father of your baby.'

'Oh, Paulo,' she pleaded. 'Please. *Help* me.'

It was the lifeless quality to her voice which blasted into his consciousness and made him decide to act. Because through everything that had happened up until now she'd kept her spirit and her courage intact. Even her tears before the baby had been oddly defiant, brave tears. And for Isabella to look the way she was looking at him right now...helplessly...hopelessly...

'Come back into the sitting room with me.'

'He wants a drink—'

'*Damn* his drink!' Paulo contradicted in a voice of pure venom.

Roberto looked up as he heard them approach. 'No drink, I see. But you've brought lover-boy with you instead.' His eyes narrowed with malicious calculation. 'Though maybe you haven't told him how *close* we were, Isabella?'

'You've come a long way, Bonino,' Paulo observed, almost pleasantly. 'Surely not just to draw attention to your inadequacies in bed?'

Roberto flushed. 'A very long way,' he agreed. 'But I figured it was worth it.'

'So what have you come for? Money?'

Roberto tensed and a shrewd look entered his eyes. 'Actually, I came to discuss access to my daughter—'

Isabella sucked in a breath of outraged horror.

'She is not,' interrupted Paulo calmly, '*your* daughter.'

The two men stared at one another.

'She's mine,' said Paulo quietly.

Only the welfare of her baby gave Isabella the strength not to react, but her legs felt unsteady. She glanced anxiously over at Roberto.

'You're lying,' he accused.

Paulo shook his head and snaked out a hand to draw Isabella snugly against the jut of his hip, fingertips curving with arrogant ownership around her waist. 'We're lovers,' he said deeply and, compelled by something she couldn't resist in that deep, rich voice, Isabella raised her face to his. 'We've always been lovers, haven't we, *querida*?'

And in one sense she supposed they had. There had certainly never been any other man who had taken up residence heart, body and soul, the way Paulo had. She nodded her head, too dazed to speak.

'I d-don't believe you,' spluttered Roberto.

'Then prove it,' said Paulo in a cold and deadly voice. 'Go ahead—apply to the British courts. You can start the whole lengthy and exceedingly expensive legal proceedings *and you'll lose*,' he threatened.

Roberto swallowed. 'And if I won?'

Paulo appeared to consider the feeble question, then shrugged. 'Well, it's all academic—because you won't. But you certainly wouldn't get any co-operation from us if you were expecting to take Estella out of the country. Even if you could afford the return ticket—which I doubt, not on a lecturer's salary. A salary you may not have for much longer.'

His eyes glittered like black diamonds. 'If you take this any further, I shall hire the very best lawyers in the land to prove that you are an unfit father. And I don't think I'd have much trouble doing that, do you—in view of your rather *unconventional* attitude to student relationships?'

Roberto licked his lips. 'I think I will have that drink, after all; then I'll go.'

Paulo ignored the request. 'Are you still working?' he asked, still in that same calm, almost pleasant voice.

Roberto swallowed. 'Sure.'

Paulo smiled, but it was a hard, cruel smile. 'How do you think that your superiors would feel about you abusing your position by seducing students? They might get mad at that, mightn't they? So might the other students. And their parents—now they would be *really* mad, wouldn't they? You see, Roberto, even in the most liberal circles, people don't take kindly to a fundamental position of trust being abused.'

Roberto had started to shake. He licked his lips like a cornered animal. 'What are you planning to do?' he whimpered.

Letting Isabella go, Paulo took a deliberate and intimidating step forward. 'What I would like to do,' he said icily, 'is to beat your face into an unrecognisable pulp before extracting a full and frank confession which I would then take to the university authorities to deal with. I would like to see you jailed and to make sure that you never worked in a responsible position again. That is what I would *like* to do—'

'Paulo—'

'Not now, Bella,' he instructed softly, before turning

his attention back to the man who seemed to have shrunk in stature since Isabella had first entered the room. 'But I don't trust myself to lay a finger on you, you worthless piece of slime. So instead I am telling you to get out of Isabella's life once and for all. And to stay out. And that any mention of your fleeting—' his mouth hardened on the next word '—involvement with her will be rigorously denied and followed up with an exposé you will live to regret. Believe me.' His eyes glittered. 'Oh, and if word ever reaches me that you are forming unsuitable relationships with any of your students again...' He allowed himself a grim smile and shook his head. 'Just don't go there, Bonino,' he warned softly. 'And now get out of my house before I change my mind and hit you.'

Roberto opened his mouth like a stranded fish. He turned to Isabella with a question in his eyes, but something in her face made the question die on his lips, unasked. He swallowed and shrugged, then turned and walked out of the room without another word.

The echoing of the front door closing behind him was the only sound which could be heard for several long, tense moments.

'How can I ever thank you?' she whispered, lifting tentative fingertips to touch the dark rasp of his chin but he shook his head, and she let her hand fall.

'Keeping a creep like that out of Estella's life is thanks enough,' he answered coolly. 'You don't have to make love to me to close the deal, Bella.'

'Close...the...deal?' She screwed up her eyes in disbelief. 'But yesterday you were asking me to marry you.'

'And we both know what your reply was.'

'I thought it was a joke.'

'A *joke*?' He stared at her incredulously. 'Why would I joke about something like that?'

She met his eyes defiantly. 'Because you don't "do" serious, remember?'

'OK,' he conceded. 'That *was* a pretty arrogant statement to make—but it was true at the time I said it.'

'And you made asking me to marry you sound so casual,' she accused. 'Like you didn't really care one way or the other.'

'Bella,' he said patiently, 'our relationship has hardly been the model of conventional behaviour up until now, has it? But if a diamond ring and a bended knee are what you want—'

'They aren't!' she said furiously. 'But maybe you could try convincing me that our relationship isn't going to "burn itself out" the way you predicted! What's the point of getting married, if that's the case?'

He frowned. 'That's not what I said—'

'It is!'

He shook his head. 'No,' he contradicted flatly. 'You asked me how long we would be lovers, and I said that I didn't know—*until it burned itself out*. But it isn't going to, is it, Bella?' he questioned softly. 'We both know that.' He saw the way that her lips trembled, and gave a slow, lazy smile. 'We like and respect one another in a way that goes bone-deep. We click in a way that's so easy. I feel fantastic when I'm with you—and this kind of feeling doesn't come along in most people's lifetime. Believe me, *querida*.'

'Then why did you say it?'

'Why?' He stroked her hair thoughtfully. 'Because I was hurt and frustrated—furious that someone else had been your lover and furious with myself for not having prevented it. And yet, I had this overpowering urge to protect you and look after you. I wanted to ask you to marry me then, but the last thing you needed was *more* emotional pressure being heaped on you. That's why I was prepared to wait—and I thought that once we really *did* become lovers rather than just fantasising about it, then...'

'What?' she asked him tremulously.

'That by then you would know how much I loved you.' His eyes softened as he looked down at her. 'And I was certain that my behaviour since would have convinced you that I've fallen completely under your spell.' He gave a very sexy grin. 'Bella—do you think I'm like that in bed with *every* woman I've ever slept with?'

'Never, ever mention them again!' she warned him fiercely.

He smiled. 'I love you.' He turned and looked down at her upturned face, at the golden light dazzling from her huge, amber eyes. 'Don't ask me how or when or where it happened. It just did.'

She reached up to stroke the dark rasp of his chin. 'I've always loved you, Paulo,' she told him honestly. 'From childhood devotion to adult emotion. But when I got pregnant I felt so bad about myself that I didn't think anyone would love me...'

'But now you do?' he probed softly.

'Oh, yes. Yes! I love you, Paulo!' And she went straight into his waiting arms.

'Cue violins,' murmured Paulo, as he gathered her close and bent his head to kiss her.

CHAPTER FOURTEEN

ISABELLA turned around, the silk-satin of her gown making a slithery rustle as she moved away from the mirror. 'Do I look OK?' she asked uncertainly.

It was a moment or so before Paulo could speak. 'You look…enchanting, *querida*. So enchanting, in fact, that I would like to remove the dress that you have just spent so long getting into—and make love to you for the rest of the afternoon. But unfortunately,' he finished dramatically as he fastened a pure-gold cuff-link, 'I have a wedding to attend.'

'But wedding dresses are not supposed to look sexy,' said Isabella worriedly. 'That wasn't why I chose it.'

'I know—but I suspect,' said Paulo drily, 'that you could cover yourself from head to toe in sacking and I would still be overcome by desire for you.'

'Well, that's good,' she said contentedly. 'Do you think we ought to give Papa a knock? The cars will be here soon and we don't want to be late.'

'I just did. He's dressed in his morning suit, and is entertaining *both* our children. Eddie loves him.'

'So does Stella.'

Her father had flown over for the wedding, and it had been an emotional reunion. Isabella hadn't seen him for over a year and a year was a long time for a man of his age. He looked older, a little more stooped and certainly greyer, but his brilliant smile on seeing his brand-new granddaughter for the first time had made him seem positively boyish.

185

And once Luis had been convinced of his daughter's happiness he had been more than charmed by the comfortable life she shared in London with Paulo and their children.

'No homesickness?' he had questioned sternly.

And Bella had glanced across at Paulo. 'My home is here,' she'd said simply.

Luis had mentioned casually that he was leaving the running of the ranch in the hands of his manager and was in the process of buying a small flat in Salvador.

And that night in bed Paulo had told Bella that he suspected her father might have a romance brewing.

'Do you think so?'

'He mentioned something about it in the car when I picked him up at the airport,' he'd admitted, then studied her face in the moonlight. 'Someone he's known for a long time—but he was waiting until you were settled. Would you mind?'

'Mind?' she'd asked, with a grin. 'Why would I? I'm far too smug and happy to do anything other than shout the advantages of living in a loving relationship from the rooftops!'

'Good,' Paulo had whispered before he'd bent to lick her nipple.

She had also told her father that she would probably complete her university degree. 'One day,' she'd added, but there was no trace of wistfulness in her voice. No sense of dreams unfulfilled—not when she'd everything she had ever wanted right here.

'She's young enough to do anything she wants to do,' Paulo had said, sizzling her a narrow-eyed look of adoration.

'That's provided he doesn't give you any more

babies,' Luis had teased, as he'd bent to ruffle the dark curls of his granddaughter.

Paulo's and Bella's eyes had met across the room in a moment of perfect understanding. As far as Luis was concerned, Paulo really *was* the father of her baby—but they felt exactly the same. He was—in every single way that counted.

She watched him now as he slotted a scarlet rose into his button-hole, and thought that she had never seen her husband-to-be look more gorgeous. *Gato.*

With a hand that sparkled from the light thrown off by the enormous diamond which Paulo had insisted on buying her—'conventional enough for you?' he'd growled—Isabella picked up her bouquet.

'I guess we'd better go.'

'In a minute,' he murmured. 'But we have something very important to do first.'

Isabella straightened his button-hole and looked up at him in bemusement. 'What have I forgotten?'

He smiled. 'Why, this, of course.'

And he kissed her.

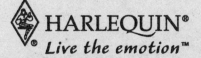

The world's bestselling romance series.

HARLEQUIN®
Presents

Seduction and Passion Guaranteed!

Legally wed, great together in bed,
but he's never said…"I love you."

They're…

Wedlocked!

**The series
in which
marriages are
made in haste…
and love
comes later…**

Don't miss

THE TOKEN WIFE by Sara Craven,
#2369 on sale January 2004

Coming soon

THE CONSTANTIN MARRIAGE by Lindsay Armstrong,
#2384 on sale March 2004

**Pick up a Harlequin Presents® novel and you will
enter a world of spine-tingling passion and
provocative, tantalizing romance!**

Available wherever Harlequin books are sold.

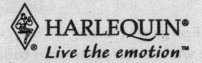

HARLEQUIN®
Live the emotion™

Visit us at www.eHarlequin.com

HPWEDJF

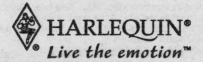